MURDER AT SEA

MURDER AT SEA

RICHARD CONNELL

COACHWHIP PUBLICATIONS
GREENVILLE, OHIO

Murder at Sea, by Richard Connell
© 2025 Coachwhip Publications edition
Cover image: © AndreasG

First published 1929
Richard Connell, 1893-1949
CoachwhipBooks.com

ISBN 1-61646-602-2
ISBN-13 978-1-61646-602-2

To the Reader

This book was written by one who loves a mystery, for the other amateurs of crime who like to find a dead body at the end of the first chapter, and a murderer at the end of the book. It is a mystery for them to solve, to compensate in a small way for the big mystery which none of us will ever be able to solve. I dedicate this book to all crime-fanciers, and particularly to Louise Fox Connell, John Chapman Hilder, Earle H. Balch, Carl Brandt and Erdmann Brandt.

Richard Connell.
Green's Farms, Conn.
October 31, 1928.

I
THE CURIOUS MAN

Curiosity was Matthew Kelton's greatest vice. It was also his chief source of pleasure. His desire to know how, who, when, where and why was insatiable. For rather more than fifty years he had peered at life with questioning, interested eyes. The failing which is popularly supposed to have killed a cat had had no lethal effect on Matthew Kelton. Few men were more alive and alert.

He had seen, in his time, many strange things. He had wandered in the labyrinth of human behavior and found it full of many dark and unexpected turnings. He was never bored. He found the conduct of man too unpredictable. He seemed to live and move about in a perpetual state of quiet excitement.

Anything which smacked of a puzzle drew his mind as a magnet draws a needle. His energy and acumen when he was working at something which challenged his mind was the amazement of his friends. Some said that had he lived in medieval times he would have run the risk of being burned as a sorcerer; he appeared, at times, to employ black magic.

"I simply put two and two together," he used to explain. "My problem is to find what two added to what other two will give the desired four."

"I am interested," he once said, "in all riddles."

"Try your hand at solving the eternal riddle of the Sphinx," a friend suggested.

Matthew Kelton smiled.

"He's simply a mass of grinning stone," he said, "the monument of some man's egomania. I am vastly more interested in why some obscure shipping clerk pilfers ten dollars from his employer. Human hieroglyphics—they are my passion."

Matthew Kelton was in the happy position of being able to gratify his passion for finding out things. As a young man he had been a highly capable chemist. In the course of his work one day he had asked himself what would happen if certain chemicals were combined with certain other chemicals. Having asked the question, it followed that he could not rest content until he had found the answer. The answer was Kelton's Night of Roses, a haunting, exotic perfume. He promptly sold the formula, invested the money, bought a small house in a quiet town outside the metropolis, and was free to devote his entire time to the enthralling science of curiosity. For mysteries he lived.

He had, in his house, a laboratory, a workshop and a library. Also a venerable Scotch lady who kept house, watched the pennies, and turned out uncommonly good steak-and-kidney pies. His income, some eight thousand dollars a year, was more than ample for his simple needs.

There were puzzles enough in the world to keep Matthew Kelton busy. Yet he was always seeking new ones. Often he did not have to look far. The police had discovered his talent for throwing light on very somber points in cases confronting them. So they called on him frequently for help. He gave it, cheerfully, asking neither pay nor credit; but only if the case was a genuine mystery. To what he called "rule of thumb, unimaginative crimes" he would give no attention.

One night—it was early in March, a singularly raw and nasty March—Matthew Kelton, at work in his library on a cryptogram whose ingenuity would have defied Poe himself, began to sniffle. He knew what that meant. The day before he had poked about in the sleet, searching for a footprint which was the core of the knotty case on which he was working. He found the footprint, drew from it an answer, proved that answer correct, saved a blameless man from a very unpleasant ten minutes in the electric chair, and—caught a heavy cold.

He put aside the cryptogram and rang for his house-keeper.

"Mrs. McNab?"

"Yes, Mr. Kelton."

"I'm going away. To a warmer climate. No, I'm not going to die."

Seeing that Mr. Kelton spoke with humorous intent, Mrs. McNab parted her elderly features in a smile.

"I'm going," said Matthew Kelton, "to Bermuda. I find I can get a boat day after to-morrow. Please put the blue suit, and the dinner suit and some shirts and things in a bag. If you want to, you can close the house and visit your sister. I expect to be gone three or four weeks."

"Yes, Mr. Kelton." Mrs. McNab showed no surprise. She wasn't exactly sure where Bermuda was; but it didn't matter. She had known her employer to depart for Madagascar and for Korea on a day's notice.

"I'll be sailing on the steamer *Pendragon,*" Matthew Kelton informed her. "Make a note to send any mail to the Royal Monteville Hotel, Hamilton. I expect to bask in the sun, and not ask a single question. I intend to take a thorough rest."

Again Mrs. McNab smiled.

"I must knock out this cold, you see," explained Matthew Kelton. Mrs. McNab suggested a hot toddy and extra blankets as a temporary relief measure. To this her employer agreed.

So it came about that when the S.S. *Pendragon* began to make ready to slip away from her pier in the North River on the fifth of March, Matthew Kelton was aboard. He stood on the deck, watching scurrying men unfasten the giant hawsers. He was a smallish man, neatly made, with unusually competent looking hands, and a great shock of white hair which billowed up above a sharp, incisive face. He looked, indeed, rather like a cockatoo. When he asked a question—and he was usually asking them—he cocked his head on one side and looked at the other person with eyes which were both friendly and shrewd.

There was the usual rush and hurry as the gangplank was raised, and the last minute visitors scrambled to the shore. Then the Pendragon eased out through the floating ice cakes, faced down stream, and with steady throbbing engines began her two-day trip across six hundred and sixty-six miles of ocean to the group of sunny islands, to make which, uncountable billions of coral polyps have given up their lives.

The S.S. *Pendragon* was not one of the regular ships which ply between New York and Bermuda. She was smaller—some five thousand tons—and less ornate, for primarily she was a freight ship. She had an even dozen roomy cabins, however; so her thrifty owners filled them, on each trip, with passengers. Matthew Kelton, who knew all sorts of people, knew the president of the line, and he had been able, at the last moment, to secure Cabin C, the choicest on the ship.

As the S.S. *Pendragon* poked her big black nose down past Staten Island, Matthew Kelton looked about him at his fellow-travelers. He had a friendly soul, and he fully expected that he would know most of those on board before the trip of forty-eight hours was over. They looked, he thought, rather more interesting than the usual run of travelers. One pair, he decided on the spot, was a honey-moon couple.

It was a gray day, and the wind was chilling. Matthew Kelton went below to his cabin to get a sweater to wear under his tweed ulster. As he was going down the stairs, another man was coming up, in a hurry. Deep in his own thoughts, he apparently did not see Matthew Kelton, for he collided with him. He was a big man, one of the biggest men Matthew Kelton had ever seen, with an enormous bright pink face and shaggy sandy eyebrows. He was wearing the uniform of an officer in the merchant marine.

"Very sorry, sir," he said, breathlessly. "Didn't see you coming. I suppose I should sound my horn when turning these narrow stairs."

Matthew Kelton, who had had some of the breath bumped out of him, said it didn't matter, and added, "Aren't you Captain Galvin?"

"I am," said the big man.

"My name's Matthew Kelton."

The Captain thrust out a huge hand.

"Glad to see you aboard, Mr. Kelton. Mr. Wraymore told me you were going to be with us and told me to look out for you, especially. I was going to look you up as soon as we were well under way. I've heard a lot about you. Hope you'll have a fine trip. If there's anything I can do to make you more comfortable, please let me know. I've got to rush now. There are a thousand and one things to do on an old tub like this. Hope you'll drop into my cabin later for a chat and a cigar and perhaps something to wet your whistle with."

"Thank you, Captain. I'll be delighted to."

The big man hurried on his way. Matthew Kelton started down the corridor. He had not taken ten steps, when he was violently run into again. This time the person who collided with him was a woman.

With a hasty "Sorry" she brushed past him. She had, he noticed, a deep, almost harsh voice, not an American voice. He noticed also, for he had a quick eye for detail, that she was wearing a long cloak of some dark material, not a usual sort of garment; that she had a broad, almost peasant-like face, and a thick, heavy-set figure.

"Never saw such a place for being bumped into," remarked Matthew Kelton to himself. "First the Captain, and now this rather Amazonian lady. What are they in such a hurry about?"

He liked his cabin. It was spacious, with two portholes, closed because of the heavy March sea, and a comfortable looking curtained bunk. He bent over his worn pigskin bag in order to take out the sweater. As he did so, he stopped, stared, and whistled. Some one had already opened his bag!

It had not been locked. He'd lost the key to it years ago in fact; but that didn't matter, since he had nothing of value in the bag. His money he always carried in a wallet in the inside pocket of the suit he was wearing. He examined the bag. Beyond doubt, it had been opened while he was on deck. It had been opened, and closed again, closed, apparently, by a hasty and nervous hand, for the straps were not fastened down. Matthew Kelton was sure they had been in place when, perhaps an hour before, he had followed the steward into the cabin, had seen him set down the bag, and had dismissed him.

He rang now for that steward.

Almost immediately he heard a faint tap-tap at his door.

"Come in," said Matthew Kelton. The steward came in. He was a chalk-pale man of perhaps thirty, with a long, rather melancholy face.

"You look after this cabin, I suppose," said Matthew Kelton. His manner was casual.

"Yes, sir."

"What's your name?"

"Larsen, sir."

"Scandinavian?"

"Swede, sir."

"Larsen," asked Matthew Kelton, cocking his head on one side, "is it part of a steward's duty on this ship to open the passenger's baggage?"

"No, sir. We have orders never to do that unless we are asked to."

"I see. You haven't been in my cabin since I left, have you?"

"No, sir."

"Now that is rather odd," said Matthew Kelton, softening his words by appearing to talk partly to himself. "While I was up on deck, somebody opened my bag, and closed it again."

"It wasn't me, sir."

"I think," said Matthew Kelton, "I'd better look inside."

He made a swift examination of the contents of his bag. Nothing—not a thing—had been taken; but somebody had pawed through that bag. He turned to the steward who had been watching him with anxious eyes.

"It's all right, Larsen," he said. "Nothing missing. Perhaps somebody made a mistake and got into the wrong cabin. They do look very much alike. You may go."

"Yes, sir.

The steward started for the door. Matthew Kelton stopped him with a question.

"I hope you won't mind my asking you something rather personal," he said.

"No, sir."

"Do you use perfume?"

Something like a grin flickered across the pale face.

"Never, sir."

"Very well. That's all, thank you."

The steward left. Matthew Kelton sat on the edge of his bunk and ran his fingers through his shock of hair. Here was a puzzle, a minor one, to be sure, but nevertheless a puzzle. For his nostrils, trained in such matters, had detected something in that room, something so faint it might have escaped less sensitive nostrils. It was the unmistakable odor of perfume. Matthew Kelton could not be entirely sure, but it seemed to him that it might very well be some of the perfume he had discovered, Night of Roses. He never carried any with him, himself; but someone who did use it had been in that cabin—and not long ago.

He looked out of his cabin door. The door of Cabin B, across the corridor, was tight closed, and he heard no sound in there. The only sounds he could hear were the creaking and straining of the ship, and the dull beat of the engine's pulse.

Kelton was a fairly good sailor. He donned a sweater and his heavy ulster and cap, and went up to the deck. The wind, however, was too much for him. It drove him indoors. He found a quiet alcove in the small lounge, and drew from his pocket the cryptogram he had been working on. Engaged in the task of solving it, he was oblivious to everything else. Twilight had come to the ocean, and the S. S. *Pendragon* was well out of sight of land before Matthew Kelton put down the cryptogram with a satisfied sigh. No more puzzles now for weeks. Just rest.

He went down to his cabin, thinking to take a short nap before dinner. He had just stretched himself on his berth when there was a tap at the door. It was Larsen, the steward. His manner was that of a man trying hard to keep a grip on his nerve. Kelton noticed that one of his hands was bandaged.

"Captain Galvin would like to know, sir," said the steward, in a jerky voice, "if you will come to his cabin at once. He said to tell you, sir, that it's urgent."

Kelton was suddenly wide awake.

"He said it was urgent?" said Matthew Kelton.

"Yes, sir."

"Dear me, I wonder if anything is the matter."

He looked quickly at Larsen. The man was trembling.

"I'll go to the captain at once," said Matthew Kelton.

He saw, the instant he entered Captain Galvin's cabin, that something was the matter; very much the matter, to judge by the lines of concern which showed on the captain's expanse of face.

"Have a seat, Mr. Kelton," said the captain. "I asked you to come here because I think you may be able to help me. I'm in a wicked jam."

"What's wrong, Captain?"

"This is an ill-fated ship," said the captain. "And, of course, whatever happens aboard I catch hell for it. Well, the worst sort of thing has happened. A man has been found dead in Cabin B . . . and, Mr. Kelton, there isn't a doubt in the world that he was murdered!"

2

THE TRAGEDY IN CABIN B

Matthew Kelton let out his breath in a long whistle.

"Murdered?" he repeated. "Are you sure, Captain?"

"It certainly looks that way," said Captain Galvin grimly. "Murdered he was, and not so very long ago, either."

His sigh was very nearly a groan.

"Lord, it would have to happen on my ship," he exclaimed. "I've been sailing the seas for thirty-two years, but I never before carried an uncaught murderer. A sweet trip for all hands, this is going to be."

"Maybe," said Matthew Kelton, "he won't go uncaught very long. After all, he'll find it rather difficult to escape—unless he jumps overboard."

"But, look here, man," said the Captain. "We're due to dock in Hamilton at noon day after to-morrow. We have just forty hours and forty minutes to catch our man. Once we get to Bermuda we can't keep everyone on board, you know."

"I'll help you, if I can," Matthew Kelton promised. "But, first, tell me all the facts you have. Don't omit anything, no matter how small or insignificant it may seem to you. I've known a man to be hanged because he forgot to dot one i."

"Larsen, one of the stewards, found him," said the Captain. "Not half an hour ago."

"At exactly what time?"

"Five minutes past six."

"Go on, please."

"Larsen went to Cabin B at that time as part of his routine duty, to bring fresh towels and to see that the portholes were closed. He tapped at the door, and getting no answer, and seeing that the lights were out, he went in. He thought the cabin empty; but, as he was going out, he noticed that the curtains of the bunk were closed. He had a feeling, he said, that the passenger was in there, probably asleep. Larsen said 'I'm sorry if I disturbed you, sir.' He received no reply. He says he decided to go out leaving the man asleep, when a lurch of the ship threw him against the glass rack over the washbowl. Larsen cut his hand, and the rack crashed down making a sound loud enough to wake the dead, you'd think. But it didn't wake this man. Larsen, who is an intelligent, observant sort of fellow, sensed that something was wrong—and drew back the curtains of the bunk. Well, he saw something mighty ghastly—"

"Yes?"

"There lay the man, fully dressed on his bunk. His head had been beaten in, crushed the way you'd crush a grape. Larsen ran for Doctor Charlesworth, the ship's doctor, at once, and Doctor Charlesworth came there on the run; but the poor fellow was beyond a doctor's aid. He was quite dead."

"Who was he?" queried Matthew Kelton.

"His name, according to the passenger list, was Samuel P. Cleghorn, of New York City."

"Why do you say 'according to the passenger list,' Captain?" asked Matthew Kelton quickly.

"Oh, I just meant—well, you see, sometimes men travel under names not their own. We have no way of checking up. You don't have to get a passport to go to Bermuda, you know."

"Any other information about him?"

"Very little. He was a well dressed, apparently prosperous man in the middle forties, I should say—but you'll see for yourself."

"I intend to," said Matthew Kelton. "Haven't you any other line on him—I mean his business, friends, anything like that?"

"In his card-case," the captain answered, "were some business cards, with his own name, and the name of a firm with offices on South Street, New York City. Here's one of them." He passed it to Matthew Kelton. It was an ordinary, engraved business card,

Samuel P. Cleghorn
CLEGHORN, ROE AND BECKER
Java Building, South Street
New York City.

Matthew Kelton studied the card.

"Seems to me I've heard of that firm. Wait a second. Java Building. South Street. That's the wholesale coffee, tea and spice district. Seems to me that one of the odd facts I've stored up in my brain is that Cleghorn, Roe and Becker are one of the biggest and oldest wholesale coffee houses in the city. Yes, I'm quite sure that's it. Mr. Cleghorn, I judge, was head of the company. Well, that's something. Captain, can you tell me anything more?"

"Not very much. Only that Mr. Cleghorn was alive and well when he came aboard, and up to within an hour of when Larsen found him."

"How do you know that?"

"Well, first of all, Mr. Gates, the purser, remembers distinctly taking the dead man's ticket when he came aboard. There was some little mix-up about the rooms. Mr. Cleghorn had at first been assigned Cabin C—but the boss sent word he wanted that reserved for you, Mr. Kelton; so we changed Mr. Cleghorn's ticket. He did not object. The cabins are practically the same, you know. Larsen took Mr. Cleghorn's luggage to Cabin B—he had two large heavy suitcases and a golf bag. Larsen asked Mr. Cleghorn if there was anything he could do for him, and Mr. Cleghorn said he guessed not at the moment, but he would ring if he wanted anything. He did ring about five o'clock when we were well off Sandy Hook. Larsen went to his door and knocked, and Mr. Cleghorn said, 'Never mind, steward. I won't need you, after all.' So Larsen went away."

"I see. Did Larsen notice anything particular about him, as if he were agitated, or perhaps afraid?"

"I questioned Larsen on that point. He said that Mr. Cleghorn's tone struck him as rather irritated—but stewards are accustomed to irritated people, especially if they're feeling the motion of the sea a bit, so he paid no special attention to it."

"Now tell me about Larsen."

"I can't tell you very much. This is only his second trip with us. He signed on in New York, as a room steward, a month ago. First name, Emil—a Swede. Six years experience on Swedish and Dutch boats. Knows his job thoroughly. Struck me as rather more intelligent than most men in his line of work. On duty, he did his job well. Off duty, he kept rather to himself. He had charge of Cabins A, B, C, D, E, and F—all single rooms, except cabin A."

"What cabins adjoin B?"

"Cabin C is across the hall, as you know. Cabins D and E are inside rooms on the same corridor as B. Cabin A adjoins B, but it is on the next corridor."

Kelton nodded.

"I see. I'll want a passenger list, of course."

"Here's one."

"Can you tell me anything about these people?"

"Very little. They're simply names to me," replied the captain.

"Well, tell me what little you can. To make a beginning, what do you know about Miss Esther Yate and Miss Julia Royd, who are in Cabin A?"

Matthew Kelton, who always watched a man's eyes when he was talking to him, thought, that for an instant, there was a gleam of something in the captain's. Ever so slightly, they narrowed.

"Miss Yate," said the captain—his manner was off-hand—"is an invalid, going to Bermuda for her health. I don't know what ails her—a nervous breakdown, I guess. Anyway, she came aboard in an invalid chair and was wheeled down to her cabin."

"How old is she?"

"Couldn't say. She might be thirty. She might be past fifty. She's a strange, faded sort of woman."

"And the other—Miss Royd."

"Oh, she's the nurse."

"What is she like?"

The captain hesitated.

"Oh, the regular trained nurse type, I guess," he said. "Big, rather plain."

"Does she wear a cape?"

"Why, yes, I believe she did have a cape, or a cloak on—dark blue, I think."

"Now tell me about the people in Cabin D and E."

Captain Galvin glanced at his list.

"Cabin D," he read, "Mr. Russell Sangerson, of New York. Young fellow. Tall, well set up. Looks as if he hadn't been out of college long. Cabin E— Miss Pauline Imlay, of Philadelphia. A remarkably pretty girl—blonde—around twenty."

"Those are all the cabins on that deck, aren't they?"

"Yes. The others are on the deck above."

"We'll go over those names later. Now, I suppose, we'd better face the rather grisly duty of going down and looking over Cabin B."

"I suppose so," said Captain Galvin, gloomily.

"By the way, Captain, tell me this: is there anyone in your crew who, for any reason, might do a thing like this?"

"That's a stiff question, Mr. Kelton. Certainly there's no one I have any reason to suspect. We carry a short crew. We're undermanned. There are eight officers, besides myself, and forty-one men. The officers I think I can pretty well vouch for. They've all been with me in this ship for years. Besides, all of them had to be at their posts of duty while we were getting out of the harbor and into the open sea. I know none of them were away from their posts between five and six, because I made the rounds; and, remember, Mr. Kelton, it was some time between five and six that Mr. Cleghorn was murdered."

"What about the crew?"

"They're English and Scotch mostly, and veterans of the service. I've never had any trouble with them. We carry also half a dozen Bermuda natives for heavy work—but they are the simplest, gentlest lot you ever met. Too lazy, I'd say, to do a job like this. It isn't in their line at all."

"It's a confoundedly difficult case you've brought me into, Captain," said Matthew Kelton. "We have the haystack, and we know there is a needle, and we've got to find it—but in the meantime the *Pendragon* is ploughing along toward port, and the hours are flying past. Let's go down to Cabin B."

"Right."

As they made their way below, Captain Galvin said, in a whisper. "I'm doing my best to keep this thing hushed up. It will get out, soon enough, Heaven knows. You can't keep a secret like this on shipboard. But as yet the only people who know about it are you, I, Larsen and Doctor Charlesworth."

"And at least one other person," said Matthew Kelton.

"Yes. We mustn't forget him," said the captain.

Dr. Charlesworth was waiting for them in Cabin B. He was a stout, dyspeptic looking man with a pessimistic manner.

"I just opened the porthole," he said, after being introduced to Matthew Kelton. "It was infernally stuffy in here, with the heater on full blast. Otherwise, I've touched nothing."

"That's good," said Matthew Kelton. "Now, I'll take a thorough look around. It may take me some time. But, first, Doctor, tell me about this poor fellow's wounds."

"He was thoroughly smashed, I'll say that," said the doctor. "Probably with some heavy instrument, like a thick lead pipe, or long wrench. He was struck a number of times. The first blow probably stunned him, may have killed him even. Then the man who did it made sure of his job. He was no weakling, whoever he was. Only a strong man could hit such terrific blows. Mr. Cleghorn was not the sort of man to submit to a beating meekly, either. You can tell that by looking at him."

Matthew Kelton bent over, and shook his head.

"He was an unusually powerful man," he said. "Look at that chest. He was fit, too. No surplus weight. I'd say he scaled a hundred and ninety, wouldn't you, Doctor?"

"At least that. Look at those big hands. He'd done hard work at some time in his life. A tough customer to battle with, and that's no lie," said the doctor.

Kelton shot out a question.

"You say he hasn't been touched since his body was found?"

"I made an examination, of course," said the doctor. "Not that one was necessary."

"How about his pockets?"

"I looked in his wallet," spoke up Captain Galvin. "Wanted to find out his address so I could get in touch with his friends. I put back everything just as I found it. I kept only the card I showed you."

Matthew Kelton drew out of the dead man's pocket a pin seal wallet of fine quality.

"This may tell us something," he said. He examined its contents.

"A receipted tailor's bill. That tells us that Mr. Cleghorn was not a poor man. It's from the most expensive tailor in New York. A calendar. Nothing much there. And money."

He counted it. Thirteen one-hundred-dollar bills.

"That tells us something highly important," he said. "If robbery had been the motive, the thief surely would not have overlooked this. Besides, Mr. Cleghorn still has his watch and a rather costly looking ruby ring. No, this is no simple case of greed, no murder for profit in its most elementary form. Don't forget that whoever killed Mr. Cleghorn apparently had plenty of time to search him—if he wished to. He was a cool hand, too. He stopped long enough to draw the curtains after he had beaten his man to death. In fact, I think he carefully lifted him from the floor, placed him on the bunk, and—yes—see that towel—washed his hands—"

He looked at the watch in the dead man's vest pocket. As he looked, there was a sudden marked concentration in his face. He replaced it.

"Nothing much there. The watch is still going. An old-fashioned repeater of English make. Perhaps a family heirloom. That may mean something, or nothing at all. Sometimes, I have discovered, the roots of a mystery go back a great many years. Did Larsen say the portholes were closed when he found the body?"

"Yes; tight closed," answered Captain Galvin.

"Could they be opened from the outside?"

"Impossible. Besides, it would be a mighty spry and slim man who could climb down the side of a ship and through a porthole, even if it was wide open."

"Captain, I don't suppose you are carrying a menagerie in your hold?"

"That's a funny question, Mr. Kelton."

"I'd really like to know."

"It's funny, Mr. Kelton, because, oddly enough, on our last trip north that's exactly what we did carry."

Matthew Kelton's eye shone with excitement.

"You did?" he exclaimed. "How did that happen?"

"We made a special run last time," Captain Galvin explained, "putting in at Yucatan, and stopping at Haiti. There we picked up Professor Tyne's South American expedition, what was left of it after it was shipwrecked. You know about him, I expect—the man sent out by the Natural History Museum to explore that new plateau up in the Amazon jungles?"

Matthew Kelton nodded.

"And you transported some of his animals?" he asked.

The captain laughed drily.

"I'll say we did. We turned the old skiff into a blooming Noah's Ark. The professor had captured a lot of weird animals, some never seen before, he said. Monkeys? Lord save us, man, he had dozens of 'em, all shapes, colors and sizes. They got out and raised hell all over the ship. I had to kick a big black one out of my cabin one night. And flying squirrels! Some of them as big as tomcats. And a slew of other funny looking beasts, anteaters, jaguars and the like. As for snakes, he had the finest collection a man ever saw except in the D.T.'s. Some no bigger than your finger. Others the size of a stove-pipe. I'll tell you I breathed easier when we swung the last cage of them ashore."

"Where were they sent?" asked Matthew Kelton.

"Out to Professor Tyne's house in Silvermine, Connecticut. He keeps a sort of private zoo out there, I believe." The captain's tone contained a trace of impatience. Matthew Kelton detected it.

"Captain," he said, "I see you think I may be wasting precious time with apparently irrelevant questions. I try not to do that. Believe me, I realize that speed is a most important element in this case. However, I'll have to do things in my own way. We're up against a dark business here, and every ray of light, no matter how feeble, will help us. It is my job to find those rays of light."

"Right, Mr. Kelton. I stand ready to cooperate with you in any way I can. You do what you think best."

"Very good. First of all, do not broadcast the news of this crime among the passengers. They'll all be at dinner, I suppose?"

"Yes. Unless this choppy sea has knocked some of them out. We all eat at one big table, the doctor, the purser and I and the twelve passengers. It's the boss's idea of making the passengers feel at home."

It was evident from the captain's voice that it was not his idea.

"I see. Dinner at seven?"

"Yes, in fifteen minutes."

"I'll want your authority to use the wireless for any messages I need to send," said Matthew Kelton.

"The ship is yours, Mr. Kelton. I'll notify Haley, the wireless operator, to place himself at your disposal."

"Thank you. Now, I'd like to have a few moments alone in the cabin."

The captain and the ship's doctor withdrew.

As soon as the cabin door had closed on the captain's broad back, Matthew Kelton did four things.

First, he opened the suitcases of the dead man. One was neatly packed with shirts, pajamas, shoes—the ordinary equipment of a well-to-do man on a voyage. The other suitcase held Matthew Kelton's attention. It had been opened and rummaged through hastily. It contained two expensive suits of clothes, some handkerchiefs, neckties and other dress accessories, four recent novels which showed that Mr. Cleghorn had no very lofty taste in reading, and a rather elaborate leather dressing case. That case had been dug up from the bottom of the pile of garments, opened, and thrown on top again. It was one of those cases with a number of pockets, one for a razor, one for a toothbrush, one for a shaving stick, etc. All these various toilet articles were in place. One pocket, though, was empty. A golf bag, full of clubs, stood in a corner. Matthew Kelton examined them carefully.

"They tell nothing," muttered Matthew Kelton. "Except, perhaps, that Cleghorn was going on an ordinary business man's vacation trip. A man running away from something does not usually take his golf sticks with him."

The second thing Matthew Kelton, left alone in the cabin, did was to examine again the dead man's watch. He paid particular attention to the inside cover. It was a thick, heavy gold watch, not at all like the slender, open-face modern timepieces.

The third thing Matthew Kelton did was to bend over the wash-stand, and from the thin wooden rail which ran down the side of it, take a small tuft of hair, which had caught there. This he carefully put in an envelope and stored in his pocket.

The fourth thing he did was to go about the cabin— sniffing the air.

Then he took out a small red notebook and with a fountain pen wrote:

"Memo. Cleghorn case.

"Some questions to be answered.

"Why is Captain Galvin, a hardy old sea-dog, so much more nervous than the situation seems to warrant?

"Who opened Cleghorn's suitcase? Was it the owner himself? Was it someone else? If someone else, why was he interested only in the dressing case? Did that empty pocket contain something? What?

"Who opened Cleghorn's watch, and did not know how to close it properly again? Obviously, not its owner. Who, then? Why had the original initials in the watch 'J. M' been scraped out, but not entirely obliterated, by some hand not too expert in such matters?

"Why was a man named Samuel P. Cleghorn carrying the watch of somebody whose initials were 'J. M.'? Who had hastily torn out a picture that had been in that watch, leaving a scrap of photographic paper caught in the hinge?

"What did that tuft of hair signify? Since it could hardly be human hair, from what animal did it come? It was long, strong, tough, brindled. Clearly it was not from a dog or cat.

"What did the scent in the cabin mean? Somebody—who used a strong perfume—had been in that cabin this afternoon. Who?"

Matthew Kelton read over his list of questions. He sighed, but it was the sigh of a contented man. He had a job cut out for him, and it was to his liking.

Suddenly he leaped to his feet, with a startled cry. A violent sound had hit his ears. Then he laughed. It was only the brassy clangor of the dinner gong, summoning the passengers to dinner.

He started for the dining room. He anticipated one of the most interesting meals of his life. Not because of the cuisine. The cooking on a ship of the type of the *Pendragon*

would be sure to be middle-class English—a lot of potatoes, meat, cabbage suet pudding, boiled in a blanket. But
he would sit down to table with thirteen people—if they
all appeared—and there was more than an even chance
that one of those people had but a short time before committed a murder.

3

A Feast—with a Skeleton

Eleven persons sat down to dinner in the snug dining saloon of the S. S. *Pendragon* that night.

Captain Galvin sat at the end of the long table. Matthew Kelton, at his own request, sat at the other end. He wanted to sit where he could see the faces of the other passengers.

It was a practice of his to do what he called "putting a frame on the picture." He always sought to narrow down his field of investigation from the general to the specific. He had decided that the human beings on the ship could be divided into two classes; the passengers; and the crew, including the officers. One class at a time, he said to himself. The murderer of Samuel P. Cleghorn might, of course, be in either class. Matthew Kelton considered it more likely, however, that he would be found among the passengers. His facts to support this theory were extremely weak, he granted. Indeed, it was more an intuitive feeling than a real theory. At best it was little more than a starting point.

He reached his seat before any of the others had come to the table. Captain Galvin hurried in and it was plain that he was trying to be jovial and unconcerned, and that it was costing him an effort. With him were Dr. Charlesworth, and Mr. Gates, the purser. The doctor seemed apathetic.

His manner seemed to say that it would be unprofessional
for a medical man to show much excitement over one dead
body. Matthew Kelton made a quick mental summary of
him—a lazy man, and not too ambitious—or he would be
in private practice and not filling a sinecure as a ship's doctor on a small boat—a rather morose type, and, to judge
from his face, a fairly hard drinker. Mr. Gates, evidently,
had not yet been told the bad news. He was young, with
a wispy blond moustache, and when he talked he lisped,
and when he laughed he tittered. Matthew Kelton decided
at once it was pretty safe to eliminate him as a possibility.
He did not entirely eliminate him; that was against his
philosophy. The typical murderer, in the popular mind, is
a scowling, beetle-browed, blue-jawed brute of a man; but
Matthew Kelton's long experience had taught him that not
a few murders are committed by quiet, ordinary-looking
men, with mild and even charming manners.

The passengers began to arrive and to take their seats.
Captain Galvin went through the formality of a general
introduction. There was the usual chatter.

"Isn't the ocean much calmer than it was!"

"At exactly what time, Captain, will we stop at St.
George's?"

"We'll be in the Gulf Stream, soon, won't we?"

The regular talk.

Matthew Kelton took no part in the conversation. As
he sipped his beef broth his mind was busy, tabulating
and assaying what his eyes saw. To make a start, he began
with the couple who had been introduced as Mr. and Mrs.
Ernest Johnstone. They were pleasant-faced young people,
who had little to say, but who kept looking at each other
and smiling. It took no trained observer to tell that they
were on their honeymoon, and that they were in a state
of rapture into which sounds and sensations from the

outside world could penetrate with difficulty. Matthew Kelton erased them from his list.

He next turned his attention to the three women who had come to the table together. Once again, it was easy to place them. Their clothes, their eyeglasses, their well-modified excitement, and above all, their speech, indicated that they were middle-aged schoolteachers on a holiday. There was Miss Cobb, who was short, plump and brisk; Miss Adams, who was thin and tall; and Miss Partridge, who was in between.

"We must go at once to the caves," he heard Miss Cobb say.

"Yes," said Miss Adams, "the caves of Bermuda are famous for their stalactites and stalagmites."

"How thrilling!" said Miss Cobb.

"I hope I may take some home to show to my classes," said Miss Partridge.

Matthew Kelton's mind passed along from them to the next passenger. Schoolteachers, particularly New England ones, he decided, are unlikely prospects when one is investigating the murder of a powerful man, beaten to death in his cabin.

He covertly studied the girl whom he knew to be Miss Pauline Imlay. Captain Galvin had described her as pretty. She was, exceptionally so, Matthew Kelton agreed. Tall, blonde, with the fresh color of a girl who is fond of sports— but—Matthew Kelton noted, her manner was strained, unnatural. She kept her eyes on her plate. She did not join in the conversation. Once she raised her eyes, saw that Mr. Russell Sangerson across the table was looking at her, dropped her eyes, and flushed. Perhaps, thought Matthew Kelton, she is shy, and after all, Mr. Sangerson is a rather attractive looking young man, even if he, too, keeps making bread-pills with nervous fingers, and keeps looking toward the door as if he expected, at any moment, a ghost to enter. Those hands of the nervous Mr. Sangerson attracted Matthew Kelton's attention. They were big, sunbrowned and strong—the hands of an athlete. The shoulders went with the hands. "Four or five years ago," said Matthew Kelton to himself, "that young man was a crack half-back on a college eleven, I'll bet, and he hasn't allowed himself to get out of condition, either. But he's much too young to look so grave and troubled."

Then, as a matter of course, he asked himself, "Why does Mr. Russell Sangerson look grave and troubled?"

That was something he'd try to find out—later. For the present he had to content himself with noting that Mr. Sangerson answered any questions put to him by the three schoolteachers courteously but briefly and in an absent manner. Also, that now and then Mr. Sangerson's glance stole toward Miss Imlay, and then, hastily, was transferred elsewhere. In his mind Matthew Kelton wrote after Russell Sangerson's name—"Possible—but doubtful."

The next passenger who, without knowing it, passed under Matthew Kelton's scrutiny was a man who, thought Kelton, was so commonplace in appearance that he almost stood out. He was down on the passenger list as Mr. Howard Westervelt of Denver. He had an ordinary, forty-five-year-old face, a pepper-and-salt suit, an unobtrusive tie, and pale blue eyes. When addressed, he answered in a low voice. Otherwise he paid attention to his roast beef.

Matthew Kelton was usually expert at placing people in their proper categories after a brief survey; but Mr. Westervelt baffled him. The man might be a private secretary, or a confidential clerk; or he might be a bank cashier; or a clergyman. He might, indeed, be almost anything. Whatever he was, he seemed entirely calm and poised as he ate his dinner. Matthew Kelton set him down as a "possibility."

The last man who came to the table came late, after the meal was well under way. That he was no ordinary person was instantly made apparent.

He had dressed in full evening clothes, whereas none of the others had dressed for dinner. He approached the table and standing by his chair, boomed out, "Well, folks, here I am. Better late than never. I hope you're all as hungry as I am. I could eat a couple of poached sharks. By the way, since we are all little fellow travelers together, let me introduce myself. I am none other than Mr. T. Taylor Mond of New York."

With that he lowered his fat frame into his seat and attacked his dinner with gusto.

Matthew Kelton—and the others—stared at him. He was very fat, and his evening clothes were very tight. It was difficult to tell whether he was old or young. He looked young because his face was round, and many chinned, and because his head was enormous, out of all proportion to his body, big as that was. He was like some giant's baby in contour. At the same time he looked old, because his head was utterly, completely bald. There wasn't a single spear of hair on its shining surface. He did not even have eyebrows.

Having drunk three glasses of water in rapid succession, and dispatched his soup with astonishing celerity, he began to talk. He had a peculiar voice, which at times rumbled, and then broke into a treble squeak. It was a voice which would have filled a much larger room than the dining saloon of the S. S. *Pendragon*.

"Great old boat, this," said Mr. Mond to the company generally. "And, let me tell you, I know boats. I've crossed the Atlantic twenty-four times. Never sick once, either. Do you know a good cure for seasickness. Well, I'll tell you one. Twenty-four hours before you feel it coming on, you go and lie in the shade of a tree. Joke. See it?"

He broke into bellows of Gargantuan laughter. The three schoolteachers looked at him with well-bred alarm. Captain Galvin eyed him doubtfully, then, apparently, decided that Mr. Mond was drunk, and that any sort of diversion was welcome.

Mr. Mond seemed quite oblivious to the impression he was making on his fellow voyagers. He piled mountains of mashed potatoes on his plate, saturated them with tabasco sauce, and ate them unconcernedly with a tablespoon.

"Food," he announced, "is man's greatest blessing. Have you read Brillat-Savarin's *Physiology of Taste?*"

Clearly his questions were all rhetorical. He expected no answer, for he did not pause long enough to give anybody time to make one.

"A noble book. Ah, the culinary art." He spoke from a mouth full of mashed potatoes. "The author tells of a man who invariably began his dinner by eating a gross of oysters. One hundred and forty-four oysters, ladies and gentlemen, each and every day. He followed it up with a few trout, a whole duck, and a magnum of champagne. That was a man for you. Nowadays we breed weaklings. Are you ladies married?"

He shot the question at the three schoolteachers.

They stammered out "no."

"Neither am I," said Mr. Mond, and he gave all three of them a coy look, "but I'm willing to be."

He drank three more glasses of water and for a time was silent.

Matthew Kelton watched Mr. Mond. The man didn't seem drunk. His enunciation was perfectly clear. Could he be put down as a harmless, somewhat noisy eccentric? Or was he a possibility? More questions to be answered.

Four places were vacant at the table. The seats were screwed to the floor; so it was impossible to remove the empty chairs. One empty chair, of course, was accounted

for. It belonged to the poor fellow who would never sit
down to another dinner. Matthew Kelton had memorized
the passenger list so he was able to tell that two of the
empty chairs belonged to Miss Esther Yate and Miss Julia
Royd. Their absence was easy to explain. Miss Yate was an
invalid and would take her meals in her cabin. Miss Royd,
the nurse, would, of course, stay with her. But the other
empty chair?

It belonged, Mr. Matthew Kelton knew, to a man whose
name, on the passenger list, read Carlo Varga. Where was
Mr. Varga? Why had he not come to dinner? Seasick, perhaps. But that did not seem likely. Save for a brief period of choppy sea, the ocean had been smooth. The S. S.
Pendragon was steady and moved along with hardly any
roll. Matthew Kelton felt reasonably sure that if there had
been any real cause for seasickness, the three schoolteachers would have been the first to succumb. They had announced that it was their first ocean trip, and that they
had come aboard dreading seasickness. That they had not
felt the least bit qualmish was pretty good proof, Kelton
thought, that if Mr. Varga elected to stay away from dinner it was not because he was seasick. He made a note in
his mind to find out why Mr. Varga was absent. The questions, he reflected, were piling up. When was he going to
begin to get the answers to some of them? He must think
hard—and fast.

Decidedly it was the hardest riddle he had ever faced—
and the most exasperating. It was almost, he reflected,
like knowing a man's name, having it on the tip of one's
tongue, and yet being unable to say it. The wanted person—X—could not be far away, perhaps within ten feet of
him at the dining table. A grim comedy, that meal. A feast,
with a skeleton—but a flesh-and-blood skeleton. Matthew
Kelton was hungry, but he did not relish his dinner. His
mind was rushing round in an enormously complicated

maze. Ten people were eating with him. Suppose he assumed that one of them was harboring a fresh and frightful secret. Which one? Narrowing the problem down by
eliminating the four women, that left six men. Was it the
big captain? The morose-looking doctor? The dandified
little purser? The inscrutable Mr. Westervelt? The boister-
ous eccentric, Mr. Mond? The troubled Mr. Sangerson? It
might be any one of them; or it might be none of them.
Their faces, their behavior, gave no direct clue. They
seemed, on the surface, very much like any other tableful
of chance traveling acquaintances. If one of them was "X,"
Kelton thought, he was a rather capable actor, with a cool
head and steady nerves.

The train of Matthew Kelton's thoughts was jolted off
its track by the strident voice of Mr. Mond, who, having
encompassed his third large helping of mashed potatoes,
was speaking again.

"Something mysterious and eerie about ships, I always
think," he stated. "Always feel a bit shivery myself till I get
my feet on what the old lady called 'terra cotta.' Anything
can happen on the ocean. Do you know"—he bestowed a
general ogle on the ladies —"that on shipboard people are
always more amorous and adventurous than on land? Well,
it's so. Shall I go into statistics?"

He paused, spoon in air.

The three schoolteachers tittered, and the men looked
at Mr. Mond nervously. But he was off on another tangent.

"Ever hear of the case of the *Marie Celeste?*" he said,
and continued before anyone could answer. "There's an
uncanny yarn for you! Lordy, every time I think of it I get
goose-flesh. She was a small sailing vessel—a cargo boat
with a crew of eighteen or twenty men. This was early in
the last century—around 1840, unless I'm mistaken, and
I probably am. Anyhow, she started out from England for
the West Indies, or maybe it was vice versa, and she never

got there. They found her, though, a while later, floating around in the Atlantic. She was perfectly shipshape, everything about her in good condition, no sign of a wreck—but she didn't have a single living soul aboard her."

Mr. Mond paused for dramatic effect, and to consume, at one gulp, his ninth glass of water.

"Yes, Sir," he said, "the entire crew had vanished, every last man of it. To this day nobody knows what happened to them. No sign of a struggle. Boat spotlessly clean. Cargo untouched. The captain had been writing some ordinary entry on his log, and had laid down his pen, and vamoosed. The breakfast had been left cooking on the stove. The men had gone—but where and how? They never found a single collar button belonging to any of them—if sailors wear collar buttons. There's a mystery for you to wrestle with in your bunks to-night, ladies and gentlemen."

"W-w-what do you think happened?" Miss Cobb asked tremulously.

"Search me. All sorts of theories have been advanced," said Mr. Mond. "Some believe it was a sea-serpent—left over from prehistoric times—who bobbed up and gobbled the lot of them."

"Oh, how perfectly awful," said Miss Cobb.

"Some think," flowed on Mr. Mond, "that it was pirates—but it isn't like pirates to tidy up a ship after they butcher the crew, is it? Others say the entire crew went to the rescue of a ship in distress and went down with it; but the flaw in that idea is that at least one man would have been left aboard the *Marie Celeste*. Some think the men were all poisoned—got hydrophobia or something like that—and leaped into the sea in a body. Then there is another theory, which I personally am inclined to accept."

"What is that?" Miss Cobb asked.

There was a strange light in Mr. Mond's eyes as he lowered his voice, and said: "It was done by a killer."

The three schoolteachers gave a simultaneous gasp.

"Yes," said Mr. Mond, wagging his great head, "a killer. Such men are not so very rare in the annals of psychopathology, you know. Monsters, they call them—blood-maniacs. Very crafty and subtle they are, too. Now, suppose one of them smuggled himself aboard the *Marie Celeste*; or, perhaps he was a member of the crew—or even the captain"—Mr. Mond bowed toward Captain Galvin—"and, as soon as the ship was on the high seas, this enterprising but insane gentleman began to go to work at his favorite pastime. Perhaps he began by nudging a sailor or two overboard. Maybe—and this is more likely—he saved them all up for one grand glorious orgy—and one night cut their throats as they slept, and finished off the rest with a pistol. Being a neat soul, he then removed all traces of his act and hurled the bodies into the sea. But, ah, ladies and gentleman, even after he had murdered every living soul aboard, still he was not alone. The pitiless eyes of conscience followed him wherever he went. Its harsh whisper was in his ear. He could climb to the top of the mast, he could go down to the bilge-water in the hold, but he could not escape—from himself. So, finally, with terror at his heels, he flung himself into the sea and joined his victims."

Mr. Mond had worked himself to quite a pitch of excitement as he told the story. His eyes were unnaturally bright, his face and great flabby hands were twitching. Matthew Kelton watched him narrowly.

Mr. Mond himself broke the tension by saying, with a chuckle, as if the idea amused him, "Isn't it astonishing what men think of to do to entertain themselves! Pascal was right when he said, 'Man—the glory of the universe—and its chief scandal.' Anyhow, the gentleman responsible for the *Marie Celeste* mystery was an original. Too few of them, these days. Think how much more exciting this trip would be if there was such a man aboard."

"Mr. Mond," said Captain Galvin, sternly, "you are alarming the ladies."

"Sorry, I'm sure," apologized Mr. Mond. "I was merely trying to be entertaining."

Without warning he began to sing in his cracked, half-bass, half-falsetto voice the old hymn. "For those in peril on the sea." He stopped in the middle, as abruptly as he had begun.

It was then that Matthew Kelton decided to try what he called "a psychological depth-bomb." He stood up at his end of the table, and rapped for order, as if he were a chairman addressing a meeting. He spoke gravely, in a low voice.

"Ladies and gentlemen," he said, "I have the captain's permission to speak to you about a very serious matter— something that you will all know about soon enough— something some of you may know about now. Please believe that I am extremely sorry to have to tell you about it—but I feel it is the only way to proceed."

He paused. The gravity of his manner had riveted their attention on him. For his part, Matthew Kelton was trying to watch all of them at once. His eyes were straining for a sign.

"To come directly to the point," he said, "a crime has been committed aboard this ship. It is a crime of the most serious character. Someone has been murdered—in his cabin—and it stands to reason that someone has murdered him. I have been charged with the duty of finding who did this terrible thing—and I want the help of all of you. The guilty person cannot escape. I ask you, therefore, in the interests of justice, to tell me anything any of you may know which may help me in running to earth the murderer of Samuel P. Cleghorn—"

He could see the faces of all of them. He saw Mr. Mond's eyes widen, and heard him gasp. He saw on Mr. Westervelt's impassive face a look of surprise and interest—and then it became expressionless again. He saw Mr. Sangerson grow rigid and deathly pale. He saw Miss Imlay pitch forward in a faint.

4
THE TERRIBLE EYES

Matthew Kelton was the first to reach the side of Pauline Imlay when she fell forward on the dining table in a dead faint.

"Call a stewardess," he directed, and Gates, the purser, sprang up to obey him. "It's just a faint. She'll come round in a moment."

He held water to her lips. Her eyes opened. She moaned incoherently. Matthew Kelton was aware that someone had unceremoniously shouldered him aside and had taken charge of the girl. It was Russell Sangerson. He bent close to her and whispered in her ear. Matthew Kelton was close enough to catch some of the words—

"Don't worry. It's all right. Trust me, dearest—"

Matthew Kelton said nothing, gave no sign that he had heard. But inside he was ablaze with excitement. He could have sworn that these two young people were strangers. They had been formally introduced at the start of that grotesque dinner by Captain Galvin. They had certainly acted as if it were their first meeting. During dinner they had not talked, directly, with each other. Young Sangerson had looked at her, from time to time, but this had seemed to Kelton only the natural interest a young man might take in a pretty girl. Yet Kelton had distinctly heard him say "dearest"—and Sangerson's concern about her was far from being impersonal. What did it mean?

Miss Imlay had almost completely recovered.

"I'm sorry," she murmured. "I haven't been well. The shock—I think I'd better go down to my cabin."

A competent looking stewardess had hurried in, and she helped Miss Imlay toward the door. Sangerson stood there, irresolutely, as if meditating whether to go, too. Then he turned away, and sat down at the table again.

"Well, what's to be done?" he said. His manner was that of a man struggling to keep his self-possession.

"We must not let ourselves get in a panic," said Matthew Kelton, in an even voice. "I suggest that you all go to your cabins, and be ready to answer any questions that the captain or I may want to ask you." The passengers filed out of the dining saloon.

"Captain," said Matthew Kelton, when they had gone, "I'm going up to send some wireless messages."

"Right," said Captain Galvin. "I've given Haley orders to send any messages you wish."

"I suggest," said Matthew Kelton, "that you, yourself, keep your eyes open for any unusual happenings, and that you instruct the watches to be especially vigilant to-night."

"Right." The captain looked deeply troubled.

"Look here, Mr. Kelton," he said, "do you think there's anything in what that big fool spouted about there being some sort of killer aboard?"

"It's quite possible," said Matthew Kelton. "Certainly, we have seen one sample of his handiwork."

"I've never carried a gun," said Captain Galvin, "but I certainly am going to pack one to-night."

Kelton made his way to the office of the radio operator on the top deck of the ship. It was a black, cheerless, starless night. As he walked down the deck toward the lighted radio room, Kelton felt, rather than heard, a stealthy sound behind him. It was the sound of someone moving quickly on tiptoes from behind a lifeboat. Kelton wheeled about. All he saw was a shadow, vague, amorphous, which had glided from behind the lifeboat, and shot out of view down the stairs. Only from the corner of an eye and for the briefest part of a second had Matthew Kelton seen it. He rushed toward the stairway—but the thing had vanished. Matthew Kelton had an impression—a fleeting, uncertain impression—that the shadow was the sort which might have been cast by an unusually tall, thin man with a pointed beard.

He turned and continued on his way to the radio room. He knocked, and pushed open the door. He was instantly seized from behind by a pair of muscular arms. Pinioned, helpless, he was held. He struggled and shouted.

"Who are you?" growled a man's voice—his captor's.

"Kelton—Matthew Kelton—"

He was suddenly released. He spun about to find a fresh-faced young Irishman in the uniform of a radio operator staring at him.

"Sorry, sir," said the operator. "Guess I made a mistake. Captain Galvin said you'd be coming here. I—I thought you might be the other bird—"

Kelton stared at him.

"What other bird?" he asked.

"The lad who was here a minute ago tampering with the radio."

"Has somebody been doing that?"

"Someone has, indeed. A fine mess they made of it, too. Ripped and tore the blooming machine to bits. Didn't know much about radios, I guess—but anyhow he certainly put this one on the blink. Looks as if he went at it barehanded, too. Some strong baby, whoever he was. Look at the way those wires have been torn out by the roots. It would take a mighty husky citizen to do that, I'll say.

Maybe it was just as well that I was in the first officer's cabin playing a hand of rummy when the lad paid a visit here. From the looks of things, he could have twisted the head off my shoulders."

"Then I can't send any messages?" queried Kelton.

"Not on this machine," said Haley. "It will be a good week's job to put it together again. But don't worry. The lad was strong, but he didn't know much. All ships carry an auxiliary radio—in case of emergency—and I'll have it working in a jiffy."

He set to work with brisk, professional movements. Matthew Kelton sat down and began to write out his messages. He wrote a number of them—but the longest one was addressed B. Hong, Mott Street, New York. He handed the messages over to Haley.

"Let me have the answers as fast as you get them," he directed. "Send them down to my cabin."

"I'll do that," said the operator, "and if our friend comes snooping around here again, I'll give him a red-hot reception."

He waved a heavy spanner.

Matthew Kelton stepped out of the radio room. The opened door made a pool of yellow light on the dark deck. Matthew Kelton saw something lying there, picked it up. It was a half-finished cigarette. It was smoldering. He went back into the radio room.

"De you smoke these?" he asked the operator.

Haley examined the stub.

"Not on my wages," he said, with a grin. "I roll my own. I know that brand though. Used to see it when I was on a P and O boat, sailing from London to Alexandria. Egyptian, it is, and just about the most expensive cigarette made, I guess. Seven cents apiece, wholesale—something like that."

Matthew Kelton carefully extinguished the cigarette, and placed it in his vest pocket.

"You know what happened on this ship to-day?" he said.

"Yes, the captain told me."

"I'm trying to find out who did it."

"More power to you, sir," said Haley. "Who did do it, do you think?"

"Perhaps," said Matthew Kelton, "he was a tall, thin man who smoked expensive Egyptian cigarettes—and perhaps he wasn't. That's what I have to find out. Well, hurry out those messages, won't you?"

"You bet," said the operator, and as Kelton left the cabin he could hear the whirr and drone of the radio.

Matthew Kelton went below to his cabin. It was a maxim of his that five minutes of quiet thought is worth an hour of hurried, confused investigation. He wanted five minutes of quiet thought—badly. Everywhere he turned the puzzle showed new facets. They all but bewildered him. He tried to consider them, one at a time, and found they ran together into a blur. There was that shadow on the deck—call him a tall man with a pointed beard. Who was he? Not one of the ship's officers. Kelton had seen all of them. A sailor. Unlikely. They do not wear soft, slouch hats. A passenger? It could be only one passenger—and that was the man who had not come to dinner—the man Varga. Yet it might not be Varga. A stowaway? That was possible, too. Was the absurd Mr. Mond right? Was there a prowling killer aboard the S.S. *Pendragon?*

From his pocket Matthew Kelton took the stub of the expensive cigarette. It seemed logical to assume that it had been smoked and dropped by the person who had tried so hard to put the radio out of commission. It was logical, too, to connect that flitting shadow—the man with the pointed beard—with the attempt to cut the ship off from communication with the rest of the world. Why had he wanted to do that? Why had he taken a very real risk to steal into the radio room and smash the machine? That at least, thought Kelton, was a question to which an answer instantly suggested itself. To hamper efforts to detect him, of course.

"And," remarked Matthew Kelton to himself, "it is the guilty who fear detection."

He must find that shadow, and give it a name. For a moment he felt that he was beginning to see a way out of the morass of questions and contradictions. Then he remembered the scene at the dinner table when he made his announcement of the tragic news. That both Sangerson and Miss Imlay were profoundly affected by it had been all too clear. Each had reacted violently. Was there, perhaps, some connection between Sangerson and that creeping unknown on the top deck? Would the cigarette be a link? Then Kelton remembered that during the meal the expansive Mr. Mond had borrowed a cigarette from young Sangerson, and it was an ordinary cigarette of a popular American brand.

Matthew Kelton was reconstructing the scene at the dining table in his mind. He gave a start. He recalled now something that he had noticed, and had filed away in his brain for future consideration. It was that as he bent over Miss Imlay, when she fainted, he recognized the perfume she was wearing. Some of his own "Night of Roses." The very first point in the case which he had considered important and tangible was that that familiar scent played a part in it. He had detected it in Cabin B where Cleghorn had met his end. He had detected it in his own cabin, after someone had gone through his bags.

"Pieces! Bits!" he said, pressing his hands to his temples. "But they must fit together. They must."

He sat staring at the floor of his cabin as if the pieces and bits of the case were lying there, in a confused jumble, and he was trying to sort them out, join them together. Suddenly he leaped to his feet.

He had heard a sharp, wild sound—the scream of a woman in an extremity of fear.

Kelton dashed out of his cabin. The screams continued. He raced out of his own corridor, and into the next one, following the outcries. They came from Cabin A. He flung open the door.

A woman—he knew her to be Esther Yate, the invalid—was crouching in her berth, her eyes dilated. Beside her was the nurse, Julia Royd, trying to calm her.

"The eyes," Miss Yate was screaming. "The terrible eyes—"

"There, there," soothed the nurse. "You were dreaming. It was a nightmare. You mustn't be afraid. It was nothing."

She saw Kelton standing in the doorway.

"She'll be all right, sir," the nurse said. "She has spells like this sometimes. It was nothing—I'm sure of that."

"It was something, I tell you," said Miss Yate, and her voice was surprisingly vibrant and positive. "I wasn't dreaming. I was wide awake, reading a book."

The presence of Kelton seemed to have checked her hysteria. She stopped sobbing, and spoke in a calmer voice.

"I tell you I saw eyes—eyes at the porthole—staring at me," she said.

Matthew Kelton adopted the soothing manner of an old family physician.

"It is likely," he said, "that it was an optical illusion. Our eyes play strange tricks on us sometimes."

"It was no illusion," Miss Yate insisted, stoutly. "My eyesight is perfectly good. I saw eyes—terrible eyes—looking at me. Oh, it was dreadful." She shuddered.

"The lights of some ship on the horizon, perhaps," suggested Matthew Kelton.

"They were eyes," said Miss Yate firmly. "The most wicked eyes I have ever seen."

Matthew Kelton studied her. She had been a beautiful woman. She still had remnants of a distinguished, patrician type of beauty in her sheet-white face, but it was also an unhealthy, almost sinister beauty, a beauty ravaged by suffering. She was, he decided, between forty and fifty, and a woman of the world. Her assurance was that of a woman who has in her time been greatly admired and loved, a woman of sophistication and personality. It struck Kelton, also, that her face was in some way known to him. He wasn't sure. It might be, he thought, that he knew her as a type, rather than as an individual. He acted on an inspiration.

"Excuse me," he said, "but my name is Matthew Kelton, a fellow passenger. You are Miss Yate, aren't you?"

She nodded.

"Will you gratify my curiosity by telling me if you were once on the stage?" Kelton said.

"What makes you think that?" she returned.

"I don't really know. An impression, that's all," he said.

"You are mistaken," she said. She spoke with a cold finality. Then "I'm greatly obliged to you, sir, for coming here. I see that you do not believe that I had any real cause for alarm. I know I did. I'll ask you to report to the captain or one of the officers my experience. You need not worry about me now. Miss Royd is here and she's stronger and braver than most men. Presently, I shall go to sleep and all the eyes in the world can glare at me without disturbing me."

Matthew Kelton's quick eyes told him what she meant; they had already noted on her washstand a bottle of the newest and most efficient sleeping powders.

"I'll tell the captain," he said, "but first you'll have to tell me exactly what happened."

"I will. And you must believe me. I'm not given to romancing, or to seeing things which don't exist. I was lying here, reading a book—"

"What book?"

She smiled faintly as she saw the import of his question.

"It was not a blood-curdling thriller," she said. "Here it is."

She held out to him a paper-covered French novel. He recognized it as one of the innumerable slight love comedies which the lesser boulevard writers turn out by the ton.

"Nothing very harrowing in that," he said, handing it back to her.

"My nerves," Miss Yate continued, "were, for me, unusually calm. I was reading peacefully when I felt a chill, a physical chill, and felt, actually felt, that a pair of eyes were watching me. It was a new and quite sickening sensation. It was nearly a minute before I dared to look up from my book. I had not seen the eyes, mind you—and yet I knew they were there. Finally I wrenched myself from the book and forced myself to look toward the porthole. Then I saw the eyes—"

She trembled.

"Describe them, please," said Matthew Kelton, with a deliberate calmness. Inside he was not calm.

"They were unlike any eyes I have ever seen," she said. "I can give you no adequate idea how malignant, how utterly evil they seemed. They were the eyes of a fiend. In the darkness outside they actually gleamed. I think they must have had an hypnotic effect on me. I couldn't move. I was frozen there with fear. I think I mean that, literally. I did not even breathe. How long I lay there, rigid, fascinated—I can't say—"

"Where was Miss Royd?" questioned Kelton.

"I'd gone out of the cabin for a short time," the nurse said, in her broad, burring voice. "I was gone not more than five or six minutes."

"Please go on, Miss Yate," said Matthew Kelton. "What sort of face went with the eyes?"

"I can't tell you," she answered. "The eyes held me. There must have been a face, of course. It seems to me that it was flattened and blurred as it was pressed against the glass. I could distinguish no features. Wait. I did get one impression, though. It was that there was something Oriental about the eyes. They were set at a strange angle, or a slant, and close together."

"Could you tell if the man wore a beard?" asked Matthew Kelton.

"No. All I can tell you about the face is a very dim color impression I had of it."

"What was that?" asked Kelton, eagerly.

"It seemed to me that the face was some ghastly yellow-green color."

"Go on, please."

"I lay there with those terrible eyes fixed on me—and, do you know, I felt an irresistible impulse to go toward them. It was the same sort of feeling I have had on top of a tall building—a morbid impulse to throw myself down, although I know death awaits me in the street below. The impulse was so strong that I had risen from my berth and started toward the porthole. Then I heard the steps of Miss Royd in the corridor. That broke the spell. I fell back on the berth, hid my eyes in the pillow, and screamed. When Miss Royd came in, and I looked again—the eyes were gone."

"A frightful experience," said Matthew Kelton.

"You don't believe me?"

"I do—in a way—and yet I can't see how it was possible. But, in any event, please don't let it disturb you any more than it already has. Really, you are quite safe. Your porthole is strong and firmly fastened, and no man could push his way through it. Miss Royd is here, and there's a steward's bell at your elbow—"

"I was so numbed by terror I forgot the bell," Miss Yate said.

"Take my advice," said Matthew Kelton, in his doctorial manner, "and draw the curtains over the porthole, lock your door, and get some sleep. I'm sure you won't be bothered by the eyes again. I'll make an investigation at once, and ask the captain to station a special watch in this part of the ship."

"That's very good of you," said Miss Yate. "I have a grip on myself now."

"Good night, Miss Yate."

"Good night."

Matthew Kelton went out of the cabin sorely perplexed and furiously curious. On his conscience was a lie—a white lie. He had told Miss Yate that he was sure she would not be bothered by the eyes again. Really, he wasn't in the least sure of it.

He went to the deck above Miss Yate's cabin. He was too intelligent not to recognize that he might be doing a foolhardy thing, and yet so absorbed was he in his new phase of the mystery that he pushed his fear into the background of his mind. Perhaps, after all, the apparition was pure imagination on the invalid's part. She was high-strung, a bundle of nerves, and the captain had said that she had suffered some sort of breakdown. On the other hand, it might be true. She had described her experience most convincingly.

There was a short promenade deck directly above Miss Yate's cabin. Matthew Kelton leaned over the rail. Below, in the side of the ship, was the dim glow of light he knew to be the porthole of her cabin. It was, he estimated, at least eight or nine feet below the deck. There were no portholes or other openings below the cabin. The eyes, then, must have come from above. To swing down to her porthole was possible—but only for an exceedingly agile gymnast, and he would need a rope, or a rope ladder, to perform the perilous feat. One slip, and he would plunge into dark waves below. Matthew Kelton shook an uncomprehending head.

"Motive," he said to himself. "Motive."

Then he remembered that he might be dealing with a mind to which motives meant nothing—the chaotic, illogical mind of a killer, seeking, without plan, without reason, fresh prey.

A sound behind him made him jump, and he turned about, his hand instinctively raised in a position of defense. It was only McQuarrie, the first officer, making his rounds.

"Shadow-boxing, Mr. Kelton?" asked McQuarrie, a stolid, elderly weather-beaten Scotsman with "seafaring man" written all over him.

Briefly Matthew Kelton told him of Miss Yate's experience.

"Well, that beats the devil," said McQuarrie. "I've sailed the seven seas for forty years, from Java to Rio, and from Vancouver to Sydney, but the likes of that yarn I've never heard. Perhaps the good lady is a wee bit daft."

"Perhaps," said Matthew Kelton. "Anyhow, I think it would be wise to station a watch near here. It will make her feel she is protected—in any event."

"I've been about here for the last half hour," said the first officer, "and I've seen nothing."

"Were you right on this spot all the time?"

"Well, no. I meant in this general part of the ship," answered McQuarrie. "I'll have this neighborhood patrolled, you can be sure of that—though I'm no believer in bright-eyed spooks, myself."

He grinned contempt for all ghosts.

"You've noticed nothing unusual at all then tonight?" Kelton asked him.

"Not exactly."

"What do you mean?"

"Well, it may be nothing at all," said McQuarrie. "But something is troubling the crew. It may be only a touch of the pip, but they're uncommonly edgy, especially the natives. They're a clannish lot, those Bermudians, and full of superstitions, and it's hard to find out what's on their minds; but something is. I can tell that."

"Will you let me know if you hear or see anything new?" Kelton said.

"I will that. Captain Galvin has given orders that we are to help you in any way we can."

"Good. Thank you. I'm going down to my cabin now."

"If I see your spook I'll catch him by the tail and pickle him," promised the first officer, as Kelton moved away.

Once again Matthew Kelton retired to his stateroom for five minutes of concentration. Once again he had barely sat down, and was trying to fit the eyes into the disjointed picture when there was a sharp rap at his cabin door, the rap of someone very much in a hurry.

"Who's there?" called Kelton.

"It's Larsen."

"Come in."

The steward entered. Beads of perspiration stood out on his pallid, disturbed face.

"What now?" asked Kelton.

"Will you come at once to Cabin K, sir?" the steward got out. "Something's happened there—something horrible."

5

The Eyes Again

"I'll come," said Matthew Kelton, starting up.

"This way, sir."

"What's happened?" questioned Kelton as he followed the steward across the ship and to the next deck.

"I don't know, sir, exactly. The ladies are in a state of panic."

"What ladies?"

"The three in Cabin K."

"Oh," said Kelton. What had happened to the three schoolteachers?

"Any of them hurt?"

"One is, sir, a little. But I think she's more scared than hurt."

Then they reached Cabin K.

The door was not opened until the occupants of the cabin were convinced that it was really Matthew Kelton and the steward who wished to gain admission.

"You'd better wait outside, Larsen," Matthew Kelton said.

"Yes, sir."

He found Miss Cobb, Miss Adams and Miss Partridge, in kimonos and curl-papers, three very frightened women. Miss Cobb was lying on her berth and the others were bending over her, with smelling salts.

"What's happened?" asked Matthew Kelton. A glance at Miss Cobb had told him that she was not at all badly hurt. The presence of a man in the cabin calmed them somewhat.

"Miss Cobb has been assaulted," said Miss Adams.

"Yes, knocked down," corroborated Miss Partridge.

"I'll never set foot on a ship again," declared Miss Cobb from her berth. "I'd no idea such things could happen."

"Please tell me what happened," said Kelton. "You tell me yourself, Miss Cobb, if you are able."

"Yes, I'm able," she said. She spoke almost pugnaciously, bearing out Kelton's estimate of her that she was the most self-reliant one of the trio. "Someone knocked me down— and I want to have him arrested."

"He should be hung," added Miss Adams.

"Miss Cobb is extensively bruised," stated Miss Partridge.

"Who did it?" asked Matthew Kelton, relieved to find that the matter was so much less serious than he had dared hope.

"I don't know," said Miss Cobb. "It happened in the dark. All I do know was that it was a strong, tall man with glittering eyes."

Matthew Kelton gave a smothered exclamation.

"The eyes again!"

"What did you say, Mr. Kelton?" Miss Cobb asked.

"Nothing. Please tell me your story, Miss Cobb."

"I went to the small writing room off the dining saloon to get some paper," said Miss Cobb. "I suppose I should not have ventured out of my cabin, after the awful thing that happened on this ship today—but I'm writing a diary of our trip for our school paper, and I had nothing to write on, so I made up my mind that duty came first, and that it would be perfectly safe to run up to the writing room and run right back."

"That was very plucky of you," said Matthew Kelton.

"I got the paper," continued Miss Cobb, "and started back for my cabin. There was just one dark spot on the way—a bend in the corridor where there is no light, and there should be one. Near it is a narrow door, which opens on a steep unlighted stair which I suppose runs down to the engine room. The door was closed when I went up to get the paper—but when I came back it was standing open. I hurried by it—and then I saw standing in the doorway—somebody—"

"Describe him, please."

"I can't. It was pitch dark in the doorway. All I could see were his eyes. I could see them shining. I was a little frightened, though not much. I simply hurried past. Then, suddenly, I was struck from behind."

"How?"

"He must have rushed out from the doorway and struck me a violent blow in the small of the back. It knocked me flat on my face, and almost stunned me. I was knocked down by a motor car once. It was very much like that. I felt him rush past me and on down the corridor. I screamed, of course, and the steward came and helped me to my cabin."

Sympathetic clucks from the other two.

"An accident, maybe," suggested Matthew Kelton, although he did not think it was an accident.

"I don't see how it could have been an accident. There was enough light in the corridor for him to see me. No, Mr. Kelton, I think that man deliberately knocked me down."

"Have you sent for the doctor?"

"No. It won't be necessary. I'm a physical culture teacher, you see, and I'm used to bumps. That's all it really amounted to—a good, hard bump. It's all right now. But it's outrageous that such a thing could happen on a supposedly respectable boat."

"It is, indeed," said Matthew Kelton. Privately he was thinking that Miss Cobb might consider herself a very lucky woman that she had escaped with nothing worse than a bump. "I'll report this to the captain," he said, "and we'll make every effort to catch and punish the man. Are you sure you can't give me some idea of his appearance?"

"No. I can't. I'm sure, though, he was tall. I'm five feet four, myself, and his eyes were at least a foot higher than mine."

"I see," said Matthew Kelton. "Well,"—he used his most fatherly manner, "you ladies have had a most unpleasant experience and you have met it with courage and sense. I feel sure it is an accident—some short-sighted stoker hurrying from the engine room, a fellow too rude to stop and apologize. It will make an entertaining entry for your diary, won't it?"

He turned to go.

"I think," he said, "you'd probably sleep better if you locked your door."

"We always do," said Miss Cobb. "Good night, and thank you. After all, life is made up of experiences, isn't it?"

"Of all kinds," agreed Matthew Kelton, as he wished them good night. As soon as the door of the cabin had closed on him, he heard the key turn in the lock. He smiled, grimly.

He examined, with care, the scene of Miss Cobb's encounter with the unknown. Nobody was there, nor were there any traces. Then he started toward Captain Galvin's quarters to discuss with him the strange occurrences of the last hour.

The captain's cabin was on the top-deck, forward. To get to it Matthew Kelton had to walk the length of the ship, along the top-deck. Matthew Kelton walked, cautiously, all his senses on the alert. He had not gone far when he heard a faint tap-tap, the sound of feet on the iron steps leading to the top-deck. Kelton acted quickly. He darted behind a thick stanchion, and flattened his slender body there, out of sight. A figure passed him, walking rapidly.

It was too dark to get a good look at the figure. At best, Kelton could only make out that it was short, squat. He strained his eyes and tried to follow it.

It was lost in the blackness. Then, in the darkness, there was a streak of light. Far down the ship, the door of the captain's cabin was being opened, and quickly closed again to admit—whom? For only an instant the light from the cabin fell on the figure, but in that instant Kelton discerned the hooded cloak he knew belonged to Miss Julia Royd, the nurse of Miss Yate.

Kelton resolved on a bold course of action. There was no time for tact, or finesse. The S. S. *Pendragon* was driving onward through the sea toward her destination. If the murderer of Samuel P. Cleghorn was to be discovered before the ship reached land, every avenue of investigation must be followed promptly and vigorously. The visit of the nurse to the captain's cabin might have no connection with the crime. Or it might have a very direct connection. Kelton had a quick intuition about people. He was a hard man to lie to. That intuition told him that Captain Galvin knew something—which he had not told. A veteran sea captain is not a man easily flustered by the discovery of a crime on his ship. His manner, when Kelton was examining the body in Cabin B, had been strained, apprehensive. Yes, he knew something—but what? And the nurse? Miss Yate had described her as "stronger and braver than most men." From his brief meeting with her in the cabin, Kelton gained the impression that this description was apt. Determination showed in her rugged face. Did she know something, too? Why had she come to the cabin?

To find out, Matthew Kelton marched straight to the captain's cabin. It was his plan to enter and find out, if he could, what business the nurse had there. As he approached he heard the muffled voices of the captain and the woman. He caught a few words. The woman was speaking. He knew that thick, deep voice.

"It's a bad, bad business, Dave," she was saying. "We must keep our heads—"

Then he heard the captain hiss.

"Ssssh, for the love of God. I thought I heard steps."

Matthew Kelton banged on the cabin door.

"Who's there?" cried the captain.

"I, Matthew Kelton."

"I'll open the door in a second," the captain replied. Inside Kelton could hear a scurrying. Then the captain threw open the door.

"Come in," he said, with great heartiness. "You'll notice that even I am keeping my door locked on a night like this."

"Yes," said Matthew Kelton, with a smile, "I noticed that."

"Any news?" queried Kelton.

"None. Have you found out anything?"

"A lot—and yet very little." Kelton replied. His eyes roamed idly about the cabin. In a corner he noticed a closet. It was just large enough for a person to crowd into.

"Won't you have a drop of some real old Scotch and tell me what you've learned?" said the captain. He was playing his role well, Kelton thought.

"No, thanks. You've heard about the eyes—"

"Yes, yes," said the captain, and as he poured a drink for himself Kelton saw his hands were not entirely steady. "And about the radio. Mr. Kelton, we have a job on our hands, a big job."

"I'll smoke a cigarette, if you have one, captain," said Matthew Kelton. He was watching the captain closely.

"Sorry, but I never use 'em. I can let you have a pipe, or a cigar," the captain said.

"I'll take the cigar, please."

The captain passed a box toward him. He seemed increasingly ill at ease. Matthew Kelton decided to play a waiting game. He knew too little to try to force the captain's hand then and there. It would be better, Kelton concluded, to keep his suspicions of Captain Galvin to himself. A man who knows he is suspected is on his guard. Kelton would wait till he had more data.

"You have some theory, haven't you?" the captain asked.

"A theory, yes," replied Kelton.

"Do you want to tell me what it is?"

"Certainly. Remember, though, it can be upset, any minute. The facts I have to date point to the existence on this ship of an individual who is daring, strong, ruthless. He is playing some game of his own—and just what it is I confess is too deep for me so far. Here we have a man who brutally murders another—and on shipboard, at that, where his chances of escape are minimized. Instead of lying low, he apparently continues to prowl about the ship doing fantastic, and so far as I can see, purposeless things. He does his best to wreck the radio. I see a purpose there, of course. He thought it would impede our efforts to get information, and to notify the police. But why should he risk his life to dangle over the side of the ship in an attempt to see into or even get into the cabin of an invalid woman? Why should he knock down an inoffensive schoolmarm? Two explanations of his weird behavior present themselves to my mind. The first is that he is looking for something—something very valuable it must be, too, since he seems determined to get it at any cost—even at the cost of a human life. He killed Cleghorn, thinking Cleghorn had it; but Cleghorn didn't have it, because the unknown has continued his search. The prize, obviously, is a big one. You'll remember that Cleghorn's money and jewelry were ignored. Our unknown is after bigger game. But what?"

Captain Galvin shook his head.

"I'd like to know," he said.

Kelton had an impression that the captain seemed relieved.

"My other explanation fits the case, too," went on Matthew Kelton. "That fat chatterbox—Mond—suggested it at dinner. It may be, Captain, that we are dealing with a madman."

"Yes," said the captain. "I was thinking that, too. Now, offhand, Mr. Kelton, who would you say was the maddest-looking person you have seen on this ship?"

Kelton evaded the question.

"You can't always tell by appearances," he said. "I've seen dangerous maniacs who look every bit as sane as you or I, Captain. They seem perfectly normal until you happen to touch the infected spot in their mind—and then they go into a frenzy. But you have someone in mind, I can see. Who?"

"I'm making no accusations," said Captain Galvin, "but if ever I saw a man who struck me as being a candidate for a padded cell it's that fellow Mond."

"He's a queer one, I grant you that," said Kelton. He was thinking to himself, "The captain is not so slow-witted. He falls in instantly with my maniac theory—and tries to cast suspicion on a man who will fit it."

Aloud he said, "Have you any facts about Mond?"

"None," the captain admitted. "Only—did you notice when he was telling that story about the killer on the *Marie Celeste* how excited he was? There was a hellish look in his eyes, Mr. Kelton."

"Yes, I didn't miss that," said Matthew Kelton. "Don't think I've been neglecting Mr. Mond in my speculations, Captain."

"I'll clap him in irons, if you say the word," Captain Galvin declared.

Kelton smiled dryly.

"Not yet, Captain. If you go about clapping people in irons because their behavior strikes you as a bit odd, you'll have us all in clink. Leave Mr. Mond to me."

"Have you had any answers to your wireless messages?" asked the captain. "I heard the machine chattering away awhile ago and perhaps something has come in."

Kelton knew the captain was not thinking of the messages, but of the woman penned uncomfortably in the closet.

"Haley is going to bring them to me as fast as he gets them," he said. "Perhaps one of them will contain a ray of light."

"I sincerely hope so," said the captain, moving restlessly in his seat.

"One more thing, Captain," said Matthew Kelton. "The first officer spoke to me awhile ago about the crew. Said that some of them—especially the Bermuda natives—seemed disturbed about something. Have you any additional information?"

"No. Sailors are a temperamental lot, you know, Mr. Kelton. They've heard about the crime by now and it may be that which is bothering them. It's bad luck to sail on a ship with a murdered man, you know. I can handle them all right so—"

A sharp, prolonged buzz, like the death cry of a monster hornet, sounded in the cabin.

"The emergency signal," cried the captain, catching up his telephone. Kelton was all eyes. Was this a ruse to get him out of the cabin? No; the captain could hardly be putting on the alarm which showed on his face as he listened.

"Man the lifeboat," he shouted into the telephone. "I'll be there at once."

He leaped from his chair, snatched his cap from its peg, and rushed toward the door.

"What's the matter, Captain?" exclaimed Matthew Kelton.

Over his shoulder the captain shouted.

"Man overboard!"

6

THE DEVIL AT LARGE

After the captain rushed Matthew Kelton. Let the nurse, Julia Royd, escape from her closet.

This was something more important.

The night seemed quiet. The throb and thud of the ship's engines had stopped. Already the helmsman had veered off his course, and the ship was beginning to circle back in an effort to get near the man who was struggling for his life out there in that black expanse of water.

Men were tugging frantically at the ropes which held the life boat. McQuarrie was barking out sharp orders.

"Man that searchlight," bellowed Captain Galvin, as he dashed up.

"Aye, aye, sir."

A long beam of light shot out into the blackness and played on the waves, trying to pick up the speck which was a human being.

With a splash the lifeboat hit the water. McQuarrie, in charge, screamed orders at the oarsmen. They bent to their task and sent the heavy boat shooting through the calm sea.

"There he is!"

The ray of the searchlight had found a dark object, far off to starboard.

"Follow the light," trumpeted Captain Galvin, through his megaphone. The lifeboat headed for where the man was fighting the sea.

Captain Galvin shook his head, sadly.

"It's a hundred to one they won't get to him," he said. "Poor chap." He turned to one of the sailors. "Who is he?"

"One of the Bermudians, sir. Gabe Fest, an oiler."

"How did it happen?"

"He jumped, sir."

"Suicide, eh?"

"Looks that way, sir."

The captain was looking through binoculars at the speck in the light.

"He seems to be trying to keep afloat," he said. "He's sorry—probably."

"He's a strong swimmer, sir," the sailor said. "All those Bermudians are."

"He'll have to be," said the captain. "Those waves don't look like much from here, but they hammer the strength out of a man in no time."

The lifeboat, its oars churning violently, was making steady progress toward the drowning man.

"If he can hold out five minutes more they may get him," said Captain Galvin.

The men on the deck waited, silently, their eyes straining to see the bobbing speck.

"They've got him," cried the captain. "Thank God!"

He lowered his binoculars.

"Wake up Dr. Charlesworth," he ordered. "Tell him to have blankets and hot rum ready—and the pulmotor."

Presently the lifeboat touched the side of the ship and was hoisted back to its place on the davit.

They helped out of it a drenched, shivering, exhausted—and above all, frightened—negro. In his struggle to keep afloat he had managed to tear off his dungarees, and

Matthew Kelton, watching him with eyes alive with interest, saw that he was a man of unusual muscular development, with the swelling biceps and thick chest of a wrestler. Dr. Charlesworth took charge of him.

"He'll be O. K. in a few minutes," the doctor announced. "No water in his lungs. Fagged out and scared—that's all."

He gave the rescued man a heartening drink from a black bottle.

"Take him below to his bunk," Captain Galvin directed. "See that he is made comfortable. We'll get his story later."

The eyes of the man rolled in terror. His face, normally almost coal black, was mottled with pale patches.

"Please, sir, Captain," he said. "Don't make me go down there. I don't never want to go down there again."

"What the matter?" asked the captain.

"I ain't going below," said the man, doggedly. "He'll get after me again."

"Nonsense. Have you been fighting with one of the other seamen?"

"No, sir, Captain. I ain't afraid of any of them. They're human. But, Captain, I see something down there that wasn't human—"

"You're crazy," said Captain Galvin. "What did you see, down there, Fest?"

"I ain't crazy," the man insisted. "I see what I see. Captain, sir, it was the devil."

"Captain," said Matthew Kelton, standing at the officer's elbow, "let's have him in your cabin. I want to talk to him."

A towel and a dry suit of dungarees were brought for the man, and when he had dried himself and dressed, he went with the captain and Kelton to the captain's cabin. As he entered Kelton noted that the closet door stood open. The closet was empty. The nurse had slipped out.

Matthew Kelton took charge of matters.

"With the captain's permission," he said, "I'll give you a drink, and ask you a few questions."

The seaman poured himself half a glass of whiskey, gulped it down, and stopped trembling.

"Tell us exactly what happened," Kelton said.

"I was down in the hold—alone," the man said, speaking the strange English of the British insular possessions, a combination of Oxford and Cockney. "I'd just come off duty and was lying down on my bunk in the dark. There had been some talk among the men that the ship was haunted. George Harris—that's the cook—had told how he was going along a dark passage with a leg of lamb under his arm, when he was hit from behind and the lamb stolen. Marty Corley, one of the stokers, said he'd seen eyes staring out at him from one of the bunkers—and he was sure they belonged to the devil—"

"The devil is a very real person to these people," Captain Galvin explained, in an aside. "Go on, Fest."

"We were all sort of upset," the man continued. "They were saying that one of the passengers was murdered—and we kind of thought it might be the devil that done it. I wasn't feeling any too good myself, lying there in the dark, when, all of a sudden, I see two eyes looking at me. They wasn't human eyes, mister. Human eyes don't glisten like that. They belonged to the devil, those eyes did. I couldn't move. I began to sweat. Then the eyes began to come toward me, nearer and nearer and nearer—"

His eyes rolled with fear.

"What did the devil look like?" asked Matthew Kelton.

"I can't tell you much about that, mister. The bunk room was black dark. He must have been tall, though, a lot taller than me. I didn't stay looking at him, I know that. I got up and ran—and he came after me. I don't know just where I did run, neither. I just ran—and he was right behind me. I was too scared to notice where I was going.

I didn't care much—so long as I got away from him—and then—there I was in the sea—"

He looked, fearfully, at the captain.

"You won't make me go down in the hold again to-night, will you, Captain, sir?" he pleaded.

"Pull yourself together, Fest," said Captain Galvin. "There's no devil on this ship. You keep your mouth shut and don't get the rest of the men any more jumpy than they already are. Sleep where you please. Tell Mr. McQuarrie I said you can pitch your bed on one of the upper decks, if you want to. Run along now—get yourself in hand. You're big and strong enough to take care of yourself."

"Not against the devil, sir," the man said, as he left.

When he had gone, the captain turned a harassed face to Matthew Kelton.

"What do you make of it, Mr. Kelton?" he said.

"It would simplify matters," Matthew Kelton answered, "if I could believe it was the devil. Unfortunately, a personal devil has no part in my own theology. We must look for—a man."

"I'll have the ship combed from stem to stern," declared the captain. "And that's no light job, either. There are a thousand and one nooks and corners where a man could hide."

"He doesn't seem to be trying to hide," said Kelton. "Make a search—if you want to—but I doubt if you'll bag him. He's too slippery a customer."

"I'll go over the boat foot by foot myself tomorrow morning," said the captain.

There was a knock on the door.

"Who is it?" said Captain Galvin.

"Larsen, sir," came the answer, "with some radiograms for Mr. Kelton."

"Come in."

The steward handed Matthew Kelton a sheaf of messages.

"I'll take these down to the cabin," Kelton said. "I'll need to study them. Meantime, Captain, let me know at once if anything happens."

"I'll do that. You can bet there'll be no sleep for me this night," said the captain.

Matthew Kelton went below to his stateroom with his radiograms. As he went he was thinking.

"This last incident complicates matters still more. I'm adrift without a rudder once again. Thought I had the basis of a case against the captain. He's big, strong, agile— and he knows the ship thoroughly. Because of his position he can go anywhere on it without arousing suspicion. Something is on his mind. What was it that Royd woman said? 'This is bad, bad business, Dave. We must keep our heads.' But—I was in his cabin when Fest, the seaman, saw the eyes in the hold. How can I connect them with the captain now?"

Reaching his cabin, Matthew Kelton concentrated his attention on the answers to the wireless messages he had dispatched.

The longest one was signed "B. Hong."

As he glanced at the signature, Kelton smiled. He was thinking of that astonishing man, B. Hong.

Mr. Hong described himself as "a clearing house of general information." New York is full of strange men engaged in strange enterprises, but the business of Mr. B. Hong was the strangest of them all. Matthew Kelton had said of him, "He knows everything, and what he doesn't know, he'll find out."

Just as it was Kelton's passion to ask questions, it was Mr. B. Hong's life work to answer them.

Down in Mott Street, in the heart of New York's Chinatown, Mr. B. Hong had his office, which was also his residence; for Mr. Hong was a Chinese. Also he held degrees from the Universities of Pekin, Edinburgh, Cambridge,

Munich and Harvard. Had he told anyone he was a hundred years old, they would have believed him; they would not have been very skeptical if he had said he was a thousand.

His habitat was in a shabby brick building, full of pungent Far East smells. Climbing the dark, dingy stairs, one came to the top floor and to a door, which bore a small, worn sign, "B. Hong." Once the door was opened—by an incredibly thin and weazened Chinese—Mr. Hong, in person—the visitor had the sensations of one who has fallen down a coal-hole and waked up in a palace. Those brilliant silk embroideries on the walls, those ancient jade statues, those thick plum-colored rugs were worth a fortune. But so was Mr. Hong. In a long life he had collected other things besides information.

Some of the information he had stowed away in an endless array of oriental boxes; most of it was in his head. He employed a corps of assistants, who were never seen. Mostly they paid stealthy visits to him late at night. Through them he collected facts—as a junk dealer collects bottles, old shoes, rags—and a man's secret must be well guarded indeed to be kept from Mr. B. Hong.

Tucked away in his apartment were the *dossiers* of many thousand people. He knew why Z, the Fifth Avenue millionaire, was not living with his wife, and he knew where P, the Canal street dope peddler, got his supply. Just as commercial credit agencies have a way of finding out pretty accurately what a man's financial status is, B. Hong had ways of finding out not only a man's financial status but nearly everything else about him as well. He was an old and valued friend of Matthew Kelton, who often turned to him for help.

Kelton had sent him by wireless a list of the ship's passengers, with laconic injunction, "What about them?"

About Mr. and Mrs. Johnstone, the honeymooners, and about the three schoolteachers, Mr. Hong could give no information. "But it will be obtained," he added in his message. Nor had he any data on Carlo Varga, or Mr. Westervelt.

His report on T. Taylor Mond read—"Rich, eccentric. Travels a great deal. Old Connecticut family. Once confined in mental sanitarium, but discharged as cured."

Of Captain Galvin he said, "Born, Yorkshire. Excellent record. Unmarried. His employers have greatest confidence in him."

His message continued.

"Lady described as Miss Esther Yate is probably Mrs. Humphrey Dyson née Esther Yate, a well-known dramatic actress of ten years ago, known on stage as 'Esta Yale.' Married Dyson, wealthy cotton broker, 1913. He obtained divorce, 1917. She left stage as result of becoming some sort of drug addict. Is now traveling with companion. No information about Julia Royd."

Mr. Hong was able to report, in greater detail, about Samuel P. Cleghorn.

"Born, England, 1881. Came to U. S. in early twenties. Nothing known about his early antecedents. Employed as clerk in wholesale coffee house. Rose to be manager in six years. Reorganized firm as Cleghorn, Roe and Becker, 1912, with Karl Roe and Joseph C. Becker. Firm very successful. Cleghorn rated as shrewd and forceful business man, with personal fortune estimated at million and a half. Personally he was not very well liked because of harsh, stubborn, dictatorial character. Had no real enemies, however, according to Roe and Becker. I notified his partners of tragedy. Roe sails to-night on S.S. *Tarragonno* for Bermuda to take charge of investigation. Cleghorn private life quiet. No scandals. Unmarried. Lived in apartment in West 72nd Street with young man, his nephew and ward—named Russell Sangerson. Rumor Sangerson left him recently result of quarrel. Cause said to be Cleghorn's opposition to Sangerson's engagement to Philadelphia girl—"

Matthew Kelton's pulse quickened as he read this.

"The ray of light," he exclaimed. "The one thing I've been looking for. Motive!"

He pushed the wireless messages into his coat pocket and stood up. A task, which he did not in the least relish, lay ahead of him. Still, it had to be done. He stepped out of his cabin, and tapped on the door of Russell Sangerson's stateroom.

"Who is it?" The voice which answered was the voice of a man whose nerves have been rubbed raw.

"It is Mr. Kelton," said Kelton, in his most pleasant manner. "I'd like to speak to you for a few moments, Mr. Sangerson."

"I really don't feel like seeing any one," the young man returned. "I'm sick, and I've gone to bed," he added.

"I'm very sorry indeed to bother you," said Kelton, "but this is a highly important matter. It would be wise of you to see me."

There was a silence in the cabin. Sangerson, presumably, was doing some swift thinking. Finally he said, not very amiably, "Oh, very well. Come in," and unbolted the door to admit Kelton.

He was sitting on the edge of his berth—fully dressed. He turned a haggard face toward Matthew Kelton.

"Well?" he said. "What can I do for you?"

Matthew Kelton believed in the psychology of surprise. He leaned toward Sangerson and looked squarely at him.

"Why did you kill Cleghorn?" Kelton said.

The body of Sangerson grew tense; his face hardened. His eyes were defiant.

"I don't know anything about it," he said.

"But you knew him?"

"No."

7
CORNERED

Slowly Matthew Kelton repeated his question.

"You did know Samuel P. Cleghorn, didn't you?"

"I tell you I didn't," broke out Russell Sangerson. "I never laid eyes on the man, or heard of him."

Matthew Kelton shook his head, and smiled sadly. Sometimes, in questioning a person who was inclined to be obdurate, he employed a Socratic method of his own. If the surprise of a question fired point-blank failed to get an answer, he employed more devious means. He had a way of asking apparently innocent questions, which gradually, imperceptibly, drifted nearer and nearer the truth he sought to discover.

"I'm sorry," he said, in a quiet voice, "for pitching into you like that, Mr. Sangerson, but you see I am investigating the death of Mr. Cleghorn, and time is an important element; so I have had to use somewhat violent devices in the hope that I can shock an admission out of the guilty person."

"You've no right to third-degree me," said the younger man, stiffly.

"No legal right, perhaps, Mr. Sangerson," agreed Matthew Kelton. "But you will grant, I think, that I may have a moral right. I do not believe, always, that the end justifies the means—but I do think that sometimes the ends of justice should be served even at the risk of temporarily hurting the feelings of a quite innocent person."

Sangerson seemed a little mollified by Kelton's words and courteous manner.

"Could you give me a cigarette?" asked Kelton.

"Certainly."

Sangerson held out a package of cigarettes. Kelton noted that he had been right; Sangerson smoked a well-known inexpensive American brand.

"Smoke a great deal, Mr. Sangerson?" was Kelton's next question.

"Very little."

"A couple of packs a day, perhaps?"

"Oh, much less than that. Not more than ten or a dozen cigarettes a day, I'd say."

"I see," said Matthew Kelton. "I'm not a heavy smoker myself—ordinarily. But when I have some weighty problem on my mind, I sometimes burn 'em up as fast as I can light 'em."

"That's the way with me—sometimes," said Sangerson.

"I judge," said Matthew Kelton, with a smile, "that you have a rather weighty problem on your mind now."

"What makes you think that?" asked Sangerson, quickly.

"Look at your ash tray. It's piled high with stubs."

The young man jerked his head toward the ash tray which stood on the washstand.

"Well, I have been smoking a lot to-night," he said, and the look of defiance had returned to his eyes. "Now, if you'll excuse me, I'll go to sleep. I don't wish to seem rude, Mr. Kelton, but I'm not much of a sailor, and I feel rocky."

"I'm afraid I'll have to stay just a minute more, Mr. Sangerson," Kelton said. "I'll come directly to the point. I think it very foolish of you to tell an untruth which can so easily be checked up."

"Are you calling me a liar?" Sangerson bridled.

"Please don't get excited, Mr. Sangerson," Kelton said. "As a matter of fact, I don't think you are a liar by nature, because you lie so badly, so clumsily. You see, I know you knew Samuel P. Cleghorn."

"How do you mean—'you know'?" demanded Sangerson. Kelton's quiet, positive manner had plainly had its effect on his morale.

"I have been in wireless communication with New York," said Matthew Kelton. "Look here, Mr. Sangerson, I'm old enough to be your father, and I've had a great deal of experience with all sorts of cases where unfortunate people have run afoul of the law. My advice to you is come across and tell me everything. I'm not a police official. I am infinitely more interested in justice than I am in the law. If it is at all possible, I'll try to help you—and that young lady from Philadelphia."

The younger man bent over, buried his face in his hands.

"Give me a minute to think," he said. "My brain's all snarled up."

Matthew Kelton waited. Then the young man raised his head, and said,

"I guess you're right. It's foolish to try to dodge out of a thing when you're cornered. I'll tell you my story—and you can do what you please."

"Very well."

"I did know Samuel P. Cleghorn," said Sangerson. "I knew him inside out, every corner of his cruel, mean nature. I was his nephew and his ward—and supposedly his heir. I guess you know that already."

Kelton nodded.

He had only surmised that Sangerson was Cleghorn's heir. It didn't help the young man's case.

"It was as miserable a position as ever a man found himself in," went on Sangerson. "Some people thought I was lucky—but they didn't know. Mr. Cleghorn was going to leave me his fortune. Yes, maybe. He kept dangling it in front of my eyes—and jerking it away again. Hardly a day went by that he did not threaten to disinherit me if I did not obey him even in the smallest matters. He was a cruel, hard man, Mr. Kelton. Ask anyone who knew him. I never met anyone who was so completely self-centered. Everything that belonged to him was just right; anything that belonged to anyone else was no good at all. They call it the Napoleonic complex, I believe. Mr. Cleghorn had it, badly. He was a tyrant, that's what he was, and from the time I was a small boy I lived in fear of him."

"When did you come to live with him?" put in Kelton.

"I don't know. I must have been a baby. I know nothing of my parents. He would tell me nothing. I was packed off to boarding school when I was a kid, and later to Andover. I had a wretched boyhood. My uncle was really a miser. He was rich because he never spent anything. He never gave me any pocket money, for example, and he bought me the cheapest clothes. 'If you want money, work for it,' he would say. 'I had to when I was a lad in York.' He was constantly bullying me, until I wonder that I have any will of my own left. The place we lived in was run-down and shabby, and no servant would stay with us long because he was so tight-fisted and nagging. Often, before I got to be as big and strong as he was, he used to beat me. God, how I hated him!"

The young man held back a sob.

"Please go on," said Kelton, gently.

"I wanted to be an architect," said Sangerson, "but he wanted me to go into the coffee business. When you're young and pretty thoroughly cowed by an older, domineering person, it's hard to have a mind of your own. I went to Yale—and I sneaked into all the architectural courses I could—but when I graduated he insisted I go into his office. He treated me exactly as if I were his possession and he could do with me what he pleased. In the circumstances, it was natural that I loathed the coffee business. It meant I had to work long hours and be at his beck and call. He didn't hesitate to censure me and humiliate me before his other slaves. Well, one night he said to me, 'It's high time you were married. I'm going to save you a lot of trouble by finding a suitable wife for you.' That was like him. He'd order me to get married as readily as he'd tell me to fetch his pipe. He went on to tell me that the girl he had in mind was a Miss Gorse, the daughter of a man you've probably heard of, Franklin Gorse, the coffee king. I saw what was in his mind right away. It wasn't my happiness or well-being that interested him. Old Mr. Gorse was a power in the coffee trade, a multimillionaire, and it would pay Cleghorn to be connected with him. Now, I knew nothing about Miss Gorse. She might be as charming as she was rich. But I did know that I was in love with someone else—a girl I had met while making a business trip to Philadelphia—the only person who was ever really kind to me in my life—a poor girl who made her living writing style advertising for a department store—"

"Miss Imlay?" asked Kelton.

Sangerson gritted his teeth, and nodded.

"Yes," he said, "Pauline Imlay. Well, I made the mistake of telling my uncle about her. He flew into one of his rages. He said she was trying to marry me to get his money. She was a nobody. He'd done so much for me he wasn't going to stand by and see me made a fool of. Miss Gorse had social position as well as wealth. This girl—he didn't call her that—had nothing. I was a pig-headed young fool. He raved on like that. For the first time in my life, I asserted myself. I said I wasn't going to be forced into marrying someone I didn't love. We almost came to blows. I left his house."

The young man sighed.

"If I had had a real backbone, I'd have quit him for good and all. But, you see, he had never let me stand on my own feet. I talked matters over with Pauline. She had more spirit than I, and I guess she hated my uncle as much as I did, although she'd never seen him, but only heard about him from me. We decided to try to take a practical view of the situation. I had no job, and no money. She had a job but it paid little, and she was the sole support of her mother, who is a chronic invalid. Also, she was in debt for doctor's bills. It was a pretty dismal outlook for us. I tried to get a job—and made the mistake of telling the people where I'd worked before. They wrote to my uncle and he wrote back that I was no good, incompetent and dishonest—which was a wicked lie. You see he did not want to lose his hold on me. I've heard him boast that once he got his fingers on a thing it never got away, whether it was a penny or a man. The mainspring of his character was that he had to dominate and master people. Then I had an idea, and I see how stupid and foolish it was. Pauline had said that I'd spent my entire life trying to please my uncle, and that I'd richly earned my inheritance. It would be silly, she argued, to antagonize my uncle now—unless he made matters really too intolerable. I should at least give him a chance to patch up our differences. 'He might not feel as he does toward me if I could meet him and talk to him,' Pauline said. Then I had my absurd, romantic idea. You see, I was—I am—deeply in love with her. It seemed to me that nobody could dislike so lovely, intelligent, and fine a girl—"

"It would be difficult," said Matthew Kelton. "She struck me as being an unusually fine person."

"She is," said Sangerson. "Well, anyhow my idea was that my uncle and Pauline should be thrown together, casually. I knew perfectly well that if I brought her to him and

introduced her, he'd only lose his temper, and we'd have
another ugly scene. So we worked out this scheme. She was
to go to Bermuda on the same boat with him. It was his
custom to go for two weeks every year to play golf. Pauline
managed to get a leave of absence from her work, and between us we borrowed enough money for the trip. I went
back to my uncle, told him I'd been a bit hasty and that
I wanted to go along on the trip with him to talk things
over. He was pleased, because he thought he had beaten
me. Also, he needed me as a golf partner. It was typical of
him that he hated to be beaten, cheated when he could,
and played a ball till it was knocked square. So I engaged
passage for us on this ship. Our plan was that Pauline
should meet him, and see if she couldn't make friends with
him. I was to pretend that she was a complete stranger
to me. I felt sure that she could win his confidence and
approval—and then it would be plain sailing for us."

Sangerson stopped.

"Go on," said Kelton.

"It's going to be hard for me to tell the rest," groaned
the younger man. "But I might as well. We started off,
and my uncle, for him, was almost human. He'd paid for
a vacation and he intended to enjoy it, he said. He met
Pauline—she arranged it somehow so that it seemed one
of those casual meetings which take place on shipboard—
and they had a little chat. She slipped a note under my
cabin-door, 'Good news, Russell dear. I'm making head-
way with uncle. Pauline.' I was out of the cabin at the
time, so when my uncle stepped in to speak to me about
something, he saw the note and read it. When I came back
to my cabin, he called me into his. I knew at once the
game was up. I had never seen him so angry. He began by
saying that the thing he hated worst in the world was to
have some fool play him for a sucker. He waved the note
in my face. He'd show me that I couldn't swindle him.

Just as soon as he got back to New York he'd have a new will drawn, cutting me off without a nickel. He shouted and swore, cursing me—and then Pauline. He called her a vile name. I lost my temper then. All the pent-up hate of twenty-four years rushed out. I told him he was a bully, a coward, and an inhuman brute. Uncle was a powerful man, and he flung himself at me, to knock me down, or perhaps to throw me out of his cabin. I lost all control of myself. I was blind with rage. As he came in, I hit him with all my strength. He staggered back, and then charged again. We fought across the cabin. I was too strong for him. I hit him again and again—"

"What with?" interjected Matthew Kelton.

"I don't know. My fists, at first. Then with something heavy. Perhaps it was the water carafe. He went down on his back. Unconscious, I thought. I lost my head. I ran away. It was not until you announced it at dinner that I knew he was dead." Sangerson buried his head in his hands.

"What time did the fight occur?" asked Matthew Kelton.

"I couldn't say—exactly—" answered Sangerson. "Sometime in the late afternoon—about four-thirty, perhaps."

He sank back on his bed, with the helpless look of a man who is exhausted in every fiber of his being.

"That's all," he said, thickly. "Now what are you going to do?"

"Nothing," replied Matthew Kelton. "Not at once, at any rate. Tell me—have you told Miss Imlay this?"

"No," said Sangerson, miserably. "I haven't had the courage. But she suspects—"

"I suppose she must," said Kelton. "Well, look here. Say nothing of this matter to her or to anybody else until I say you may. Stay in your cabin, and get some sleep—if you can. I'm in charge of this case—and I'm going to handle it in my own way."

"Can you help me?" the young man asked, pleadingly.

"I can't tell you that—yet," said Matthew Kelton. "At present I can only say I sympathize with you. You appreciate that this is a matter of the utmost gravity—and I must give it a deal of very serious thought."

"I did it in self-defense," said Sangerson.

"I'll take that into consideration," said Kelton. "Now, I'm going. Remember what I said. Don't talk—and try not to worry. Good night."

Kelton went out, and to his own cabin.

"A murder at sea," he was thinking, "has at least one advantage over one on land—for the person investigating it. The murderer, whether self-confessed, or tracked down, can't get very far away. Well, this case turned out to be easier than I had expected. It had all the earmarks of being *outré* and intricate, too. A most promising puzzle. Really, I'm disappointed that the solution was so simple and hackneyed. Oh, well—there'll be others—

"Poor Sangerson," he thought. "What a rotten life he had. His story about the sort of man Cleghorn was rang true. Then—just as he was reaching out for the first real happiness of his life—this had to happen to him. I just don't want to believe it."

A spark came to his eye—the sign of a dawning idea.

"Suppose," he said to himself, "I don't believe it! His story fits together—motive, opportunity, everything—but hang it all, it's too perfect. That girl now—she's a thoroughbred—and, if she isn't, all my years of experience in judging people have gone for nothing. This frightful thing will tear her heart to pieces. And as for him—well, I must trust my intuition, even though it flies in the face of facts. Why, even as he was telling how he had struck down his uncle, I liked him. He's a genuine, and sensitive, type. He might have done a thing like this in the heat of passion, but I doubt if he could have told of it as he did—with deliberation—and very little sign of remorse. Suppose I assume that there is something more in this case—some deep and subtle element—about which I know nothing yet? There may be no such element, of course, but at least it will keep me busy trying to find it. Besides—there are the eyes—"

To get an idea was with Matthew Kelton to act on it. He got up, and went to the cabin of Miss Pauline Imlay. He knocked, gently.

"Who is it?" There was a catch in her voice.

"Mr. Kelton. Will it be convenient for you to see me for a few minutes?"

"Come in, Mr. Kelton," said Pauline Imlay, opening her door. "I was expecting that you might come to see me."

8

FRESH TANGLES IN THE SKEIN

She had not gone to bed. She was fully dressed. Her face was drawn, and she had been weeping, for her eyes were red.

Matthew Kelton entered her cabin, and bowed.

"I'm very sorry, Miss Imlay," he said, "to intrude on you at this hour. The matter I have to discuss with you is important and exigent. That is my excuse."

"I quite understand," Pauline Imlay said. "Will you sit down?"

"Thank you," said Matthew Kelton, taking a seat. "You said you expected I might call on you? Why was that?"

"I knew you were investigating the terrible thing which happened on this ship," she said. "I know your reputation for thoroughness. So I expected that you would question all the passengers."

"You'd heard of me, then?" said Matthew Kelton, pleased, in spite of himself, although he had never cultivated publicity. "How did that happen?"

"Through my uncle, Andrew Glenning. He was at one time a police commissioner in New York you know. He often spoke of you."

"I see," said Matthew Kelton. "So you are Andrew Glenning's niece. The public service lost a competent and intelligent official when he died. I hope you won't mind, Miss Imlay, if I ask you some questions."

87

"I'll do my best to answer them, Mr. Kelton," she said. Matthew Kelton felt an admiration for her. She was summoning every last ounce of her will power to appear self-possessed. She was game, that girl, he thought.

"In the first place," began Matthew Kelton, "I want to ask you a question which may seem inane. Do you use perfume?"

"Why, yes."

"What sort?"

"Just now I'm using 'Night of Roses.'"

"I see."

"It is odd that you should ask me that, Mr. Kelton."

"Why?"

"Because I brought a bottle aboard with me—and I'm quite sure I left it on my washstand—for I used some of it just before dinner—and now it's gone."

"You're sure?"

"Absolutely."

"Have you looked for it?"

"Yes. Everywhere. But tell me, why did you ask about it?"

"I'm asking the questions," returned Matthew Kelton, with a smile. "It's merely a detail which interests me. Now then—you know Russell Sangerson, don't you?"

Her acting was superb.

"Mr. Sangerson? Isn't he that young man who sat opposite me at dinner? I don't mean that poisonous fat one—I mean the tall, dark young man."

"Come, come, Miss Imlay," Matthew Kelton said, "suppose we don't fence. I might as well tell you that I know you know Russell Sangerson, that you are engaged to him, in fact."

Her poise was badly shaken.

"Who told you that?" she exclaimed.

"Mr. Sangerson himself—not twenty minutes ago," he replied.

"You've been to see him?" she said, speaking with difficulty.

"Yes."

There was a moment of painful silence.

"Perhaps he told you why we thought it best to conceal the fact that we knew each other," the girl said, at last.

"Miss Imlay," said Matthew Kelton, "I might as well tell you that I had a long, heart-to-heart talk with Russell Sangerson and he told me—everything."

"Everything?" she quavered.

Matthew Kelton nodded.

The girl was biting her lips, trying to stifle sobs.

"What—did—he—tell—you?" she managed to articulate.

"The whole story of his life with Cleghorn, your little plot to win him to your side—and, finally, the disastrous result of it," Kelton said. The interview was torturing him, as well as her.

"The disastrous end?" she faltered.

"I mean," said Matthew Kelton, "the killing of Samuel P. Cleghorn."

"And do you think Russell did it?"

"He has admitted it, Miss Imlay."

She could not hold back her sobs now.

"Oh, he didn't. He couldn't have. Russell is the finest, gentlest man in the world. He had cause enough to fight with his uncle—Heaven knows—but he did not kill him." Her sobs overcame her. When she spoke again it was in a surprisingly calm voice. "I know he didn't do it. I know he didn't."

"How do you know that, Miss Imlay?"

"Because," said the girl, "I did."

"You?" Kelton was aghast.

"Yes."

"Steady, Miss Imlay. Do you know what you're saying?"

"I do." She had stopped sobbing. She spoke in the mea-sured accents of a person who is rallying all her nervous resources to face a desperate situation. "I—and I alone—am responsible for the death of Mr. Cleghorn."

"Will you tell me how it happened?"

"Yes. It happened. That's the way to put it. I didn't do it deliberately. You see, there was a quarrel, a fierce quar-rel between Russell and his uncle in his uncle's cabin. I was in my cabin—and I could hear them—"

"What were they saying?"

"I couldn't get the words. I knew their voices were loud and angry;—then I heard sounds as if they were fighting. I was afraid for Russell's sake— and I ran to his uncle's cabin. They were struggling in there—and Mr. Cleghorn had Russell by the throat. I thought he was strangling him. Mr. Cleghorn was bent over with his head toward the door, with Russell beneath him on the floor. Then I—I—struck Mr. Cleghorn with all my strength—"

"What did you strike him with?"

"One of his golf clubs. It was standing in a corner. I grabbed it and struck him—I don't know how many times—until he let go of Russell's throat and crumpled over on the floor. Then I ran away."

"Where did you go?"

"Up on deck."

"What did you do?"

"Talked with Miss Cobb and those other ladies from Boston."

"How long?"

"Until a few minutes before dinner," she said.

"Can you tell me, Miss Imlay, the exact time you were in Cabin B?"

She hesitated.

"I don't know," she said. "In the middle of the after-noon, I think. I was too excited to notice."

"About half past two, perhaps?" asked Matthew Kelton.

"About then, I'd say."

"Do you know what happened to the note?"

Her eyes widened.

"Note?" she said. "No."

"I'm going now," said Kelton, abruptly.

"But aren't you going to arrest me?"

"I am not. I'd have no power to, even if I wanted to—and I don't want to."

"But why? I'm the guilty one, I tell you. Russell tried to take the blame to shield me."

Matthew Kelton spoke gravely.

"You're a brave girl, Miss Imlay," he said, "and I'm going to do my best to see that no harm comes to you."

"And Russell?"

"Yes, and Russell. I'm going to tell you what I told him. Keep your head up, and don't talk. It's a black situation—but there may be a way out—and if there is—I'm going to find it."

"You're very kind—" She began to weep again.

"I try to be," said Matthew Kelton, "and I try to be just. Now, good night. And remember—keep your head up."

Outside her cabin Matthew Kelton stood for a moment, muttering to himself.

"Plucky kid," he said. "But, good Heavens, what a lot of unscientific lying is being done aboard this ship to-night!"

He returned to his cabin to consider the fresh tangle in the skein.

He had two admissions of guilt. If one was true, the other, obviously, was not. Miss Imlay's story was, patently, a fabrication. It was full of loopholes. Those wounds which had caused Cleghorn's death, Kelton was sure, had not been produced by a golf club swung by a slenderly-built woman. Indeed, it would have been physically impossible for anybody to take a full swing with so long a weapon as a golf club in so small a space as Cabin B. Moreover, he had examined the golf clubs, and they were all in place in the bag, and there were no signs that they had been used to batter the life out of a man. Finally, and conclusively, Miss Imlay had fixed the time of the tragedy in Cabin B as in the middle of the afternoon. There was direct testimony from Larsen, the steward, that Mr. Cleghorn had spoken to him about five o'clock. At that time Miss Imlay was on deck talking to the three schoolteachers, she had said. No doubt this could be corroborated by them. Yes, clearly Miss Imlay had invented her story, hastily, wildly. She had tried to guess at the time and manner of Cleghorn's death, and had missed badly. She was not guilty, but what about Sangerson?

She had lied in an effort to save the man she loved—and had only succeeded in making the case against him stronger. For one thing, she had no knowledge of the note Sangerson said she had written. Her manner when Kelton mentioned it was puzzled. There had been no note, of that he felt sure. Their stories did not agree at all. Reluctantly, Kelton was forced to the conclusion that Sangerson was telling the truth—that he was the murderer of his uncle. At one point was the young man's story vulnerable. He had set the time of the murder as late in the afternoon—half past four—and it happened after five. Perhaps he was inaccurate, or perhaps Larsen, the steward, was.

Then once again, Kelton thought of the eyes. Sangerson, conceivably, might have struck down his uncle in a quarrel—but why should he, some hours later, run amok on the ship, frightening Miss Yate by staring through her porthole, knocking down Miss Cobb, pursuing the terrified seaman, Fest, through the hold of the ship? That pile of cigarettes in his cabin seemed to be a mute confirmation of the fact that he had been in there all evening. No—the case was not finished.

"I'm not going to call it a day—yet," said Matthew Kelton, decisively. "I'm going to find those eyes."

He decided to make another trip to Captain Galvin's cabin to see if the captain had any new information; also to see if any more radio messages had come in for him.

He mounted the iron stairs to the after deck. He walked lightly, keeping close to the rail, as watchful as a hunter, stalking a wounded tiger through thick grass. He stopped, and froze in his tracks, like a pointer. He had heard a sound—it seemed like the deep, stertorous breathing of a large animal. Then a moan—a human moan, low and muffled. Kelton stood silent, tense against the rail—waiting.

The sound was repeated—the breathing—and the moan. It seemed very near him in the blackness of the sea night.

He strained his eyes and ears, trying to detect the source of the sound. Again he heard it. It seemed to come not from the deck, but from above him. He looked up. A few feet ahead, some six feet above the deck, a lifeboat hung on its crane. He was sure of it now; the sound came from there. Cautiously Kelton crept nearer. His curiosity gave him courage. Very gently he reached up, and rolled back a corner of the tarpaulin which covered the boat. As he did so, the moaning changed to a startled scream. A head—a man's head—was thrust over the side of the boat.

"If you move, I'll shoot," cried Matthew Kelton, backing away. He had no gun.

"Gollies, mister," said a voice, and it clearly came from between chattering teeth, "you give me a fright. Don't you go shooting at me. I ain't going to do nothing."

"Who are you?" demanded Kelton.

"Gabe Fest, able seaman, mister."

"What are you doing in there?"

"Trying to sleep, mister."

Kelton relaxed.

"I see," he said. "All right, Fest. Sorry I disturbed you. I guess you were having a bit of a nightmare."

"That ain't no lie, mister," said the seaman. "A man can't see the devil and jump overboard and sleep easy right after. I reckoned this boat would be a handy place to be in case the devil started hunting round again."

"Go back to sleep," said Matthew Kelton, "and don't worry about the devil. We'll handle him."

"Thank you, sir."

The black blotch made by Fest's head in the night was pulled back under the tarpaulin. To Kelton it suggested a mammoth turtle drawing its head into its shell. He continued on his way to the captain's cabin.

It was lighted, and silent. He tapped at the door. As he did so he heard a sharp bang, the sort of sound made, he thought, by a desk drawer being hastily slammed shut.

"Who's there?" asked the captain's voice.

"Kelton."

"Come right in, Mr. Kelton."

Matthew Kelton experienced a surprise as he stepped into the cabin. It was at once apparent to him that there had been a drastic change in the captain. Kelton had thought of him as a sturdy, solid type, with the firm nerves which go with a healthy, vigorous body. He had been under a severe strain, of course, as a result of the series of startling events which had taken place on his ship that day; but he had seemed, at first, to Kelton, to be built to stand a strain. It appeared to have told on him suddenly. To Kelton he seemed like a man on the verge of a collapse. His face looked pinched; his words came out jerkily; his hands played with the buttons of his coat, or he ran them through his tangled mass of graying hair.

"Any news, Mr. Kelton?" said the captain. "I've had a wireless from the S.S. *Tarragonno* saying that a Mr. Roe, one of Cleghorn's partners, is on his way to Bermuda with a detective to take charge of the case. He offers $5000 reward for the arrest of the murderer."

"That's good. I can turn the investigation over to the professional when the *Tarragonno* gets in."

"Doubt if we'll beat her to Bermuda," said the captain, "at this rate. She's bigger and a lot faster. Stopping to rescue that fellow has delayed us, and we've had a bit of engine trouble."

The captain ran one of his great hands through his hair.

"Any luck with your radio messages, Mr. Kelton?" he asked.

"Some," answered Kelton. "One ray of light, anyway."

"What was that?"

The captain thrust his face toward Kelton and asked the question in a voice vibrating with interest.

"Can't tell you just yet, Captain," answered Kelton. "Sorry if I seem to be keeping you in the dark, but I agreed to investigate this case with the stipulation I could use my own methods. I don't believe in acting on a suspicion, no matter how strong it may be, until I have tested it thoroughly all along the line. To-morrow I hope to have something definite to report to you. Perhaps I'll ask you to make an arrest. I rather fancy the idea of having a prisoner all ready to turn over to that New York detective when we reach Bermuda."

"You know best, I suppose," acquiesced the captain; but he was plainly disappointed. "So you think you have the man spotted, eh?"

"I've some evidence," Matthew Kelton said. "I'm not entirely satisfied with it, yet, though. I'll tell you this: my most important discovery to date has to do with motive."

Captain Galvin's face contracted.

"Mr. Kelton," he said, "I want you to promise me something. I want to ask you, before you make public anything

you have found out, to tell me. If your facts warrant an
arrest, I, as chief officer of this ship, am empowered to
make one, and I'll do so. But come to me with the man's
name before you tell anyone else, will you?"

He seemed desperately anxious.

"Yes," assented Kelton, "I'll do that."

The captain's face was creased with lines of thought;
once he cleared his throat as if he intended to speak, then
apparently thought better of it. Finally he said, trying to
recapture his earlier casual manner:

"I suppose you've eliminated the ladies and that young
chap what's-his-name?"

"You mean Sangerson?" Kelton said.

"Yes, that's the fellow. He looks O.K. to me."

What, Kelton wondered, was the captain getting at? In
the heavy-handed, unpracticed way of a man who usually
comes directly to a point, he appeared to be fishing for
information. But why had he mentioned Sangerson?

Kelton's reply was noncommittal.

"Most men look O.K." he said. "It's my job to find
what lies beneath the shell they show to the world. Don't
worry, Captain. It isn't my habit to jump to conclusions.
I think I'll say good night to you now. We both need rest.
I've been pretty active for an old fellow to-day."

"Rest?" said the captain, wearily. "I wish I could get
some. But how can I close my eyes on this ship? It's about
as restful as a battlefield. Well, good night, Mr. Kelton."

"Have you the correct time?" Matthew Kelton asked. "I
want to set my watch."

Captain Galvin drew out his watch, an old gold hunting case affair, glanced at it.

"Lord," he said, "it's three minutes to one."

He was about to snap the cover shut when something
fell from the watch and fluttered to the floor, almost at
Kelton's feet. It was a circular piece of paper about the

size of a silver dollar. Kelton stooped to pick it up. As he handed it to Captain Galvin he saw that it was—a photograph—the photograph of a woman, or rather a young girl—a photograph faded and yellowed by time. Kelton had only the barest glance at it—but he had an impression that the face was not entirely unfamiliar to him. There was something about the set of the eyes he had seen—in some other face—before. He handed the picture to the captain without comment. The captain's face was very red.

"Favorite niece," he vouchsafed, and shut the watch.

Matthew Kelton took away from the captain's cabin three new questions to be answered. First, why should the captain have an obviously old picture loose in his watch? Possible answer: because he had but recently acquired it and had not had time to glue it in. Second, a picture of about that size having been taken from the watch of the dead man, Cleghorn,—was this the picture, and if so what was its significance? Third, whose picture was it? Photographs, especially old ones, are notoriously deceptive, and yet those eyes were very like the eyes of the nurse, Julia Royd.

Then there was the captain's mention of Sangerson, and his obvious concern. Another knotty question.

On his way back to his cabin, Kelton stopped at the radio room. It was locked, and the operator, Haley, opened the door with a suspicious look on his face, and a heavy spanner in his hand.

"Oh, it's you, Mr. Kelton," he said, in a relieved voice.

"I came to see if any new messages have come in for me," Kelton said.

"No, sir. None for you. But, Mr. Kelton, I think that strong-arm lad has been snooping round here again."

"The fellow who tried to wreck the radio?"

"Yes."

"What did he do?" asked Matthew Kelton, excitedly.

"Nothing much this time," answered the operator. "A little petty larceny, that's all."

"Tell me about it."

"About half an hour ago—maybe twenty minutes, Captain Galvin asked me to step into his cabin to examine his telephone. He said his communication with the engineer room wasn't good. You see on a ship like this a radio operator is supposed to know all about electricity and do odd jobs on telephones, bells and so forth. Well, I went into the captain's cabin, looked over the phone, and it seemed to be working all right, but anyhow I cleaned off a couple of contact points and put it together again. Then I came back here. See that safe over there?"

Kelton's eyes followed his pointing finger to a safe in the corner.

"That's where I keep my duplicate radio messages," Haley continued. "When a message comes in, I make one copy for the person to whom it is addressed, and a carbon copy for my files, which I keep in that safe. Well, right after I got back to this room, I had to go to the files—and I saw at once that someone had been going through them in my absence—someone in a devil of a hurry, too. I checked them over—and, Mr. Kelton, the copies of the messages to you had been taken!"

"Really? Anything else?"

"No, sir. Only the messages to you."

"Tell me, Haley, where was the captain while you were fixing his phone?"

"I don't know, sir. He wasn't in his cabin."

"I see. How was the safe opened?"

"By somebody who knew the combination."

"Who knows the combination?"

"Only three people, sir—the chief radio officer of the line, who has it in his office in Liverpool, and me, and the captain."

"I see. Well, I expect you'll keep your eyes peeled m case our inquisitive friend calls round again."

Haley brandished the big spanner.

"I'll knock the snoopiness out of him," said Haley, "if I get a crack at him. If any messages come for you, Mr. Kelton, I'll send them down by a steward."

"Right. Thank you. Good night."

Matthew Kelton was in a deep brown study as he went back to his stateroom. He was up against one of the most deceptive of all things—circumstantial evidence. He put it together, bit by bit. Captain Galvin had slammed a desk drawer shut before admitting him to the cabin. Clearly, to conceal something—but what? Captain Galvin had acted as if he had some knowledge of the radio messages, especially as relating to Russell Sangerson. Captain Galvin had had the opportunity of purloining them while Haley worked on his telephone. Captain Galvin had the combination of the safe. It seemed right to assume that the captain had taken the messages and read them. But suppose he had? That still left a formidable enigma—Why?

Kelton was asking himself that as he reached his cabin. He paused, abruptly, as he was about to lay his hand on the knob of his cabin door. His quick ears had caught a slight sound in his cabin—the sound of somebody moving about, softly. Someone was in his cabin.

9

A Visit Late at Night

Kelton did not hesitate. He flung open his door.

The light was out in the cabin—but the interior was dimly lit by the light in the corridor. Kelton saw the dark figure of a big man standing there—and in the semi-darkness he could see the almost phosphorescent glitter of his eyes. Kelton's hand found the electric button inside the door, and he snapped it. The cabin was flooded with light.

"Well, well," said the man, and his voice was as easy as if he were greeting a passing friend on Fifth Avenue, "it's Mr. Kelton. Good evening to you, sir."

The owner of the voice was Mr. Mond.

"What's the meaning of this?" demanded Kelton, hotly.

"Just an informal call," said Mr. Mond. "Please don't say you're not glad to see me. I'm very sensitive."

"Humph," said Kelton. "Your sensitiveness doesn't seem to prevent you from prying about in another man's cabin in the dark. I demand an explanation, Mr. Mond."

"Oh, explanations!" said Mr. Mond, airily. "They weary me. Great men never explain. They do something, and it's done, and that's all there is to it. Explanations are a waste of time."

"I insist that you tell me what you are doing in my cabin," said Matthew Kelton, sternly.

"Now, don't frown, Mr. Kelton. The man worth while is the man who can smile and all that pish-posh. I came to see you to have a talk with you—and not finding you at home I waited—and, being fond of simple pleasures, I amused myself by strolling about your cabin in the dark. Come now, count your neckties. You'll find I haven't taken any of them. Why, sir, I have more than five hundred neckties of my own. Here—to show you I'm your friend—you shall have this one."

Whereupon Mr. Mond, with one quick motion, took off his evening tie and held it out to Matthew Kelton. Kelton was half-amused, half-angry. He surveyed the fat figure before him.

"You came to see me for a talk?" he said. Obviously berating the bland and grinning Mr. Mond would get him nowhere. That gentleman had sprawled, completely at his ease, in the cabin's only chair.

"I," stated Mr. Mond, "am a philosopher. My school I have denominated hedonistic-sybaritic-Mondism. It combines all the best features of Plato, Kant, Freud, Spinoza, Nietzsche and Dewey, with some exotic trimmings of my own—"

"It is getting rather late, Mr. Mond," said Matthew Kelton.

"Pray don't hurry me," said Mr. Mond, affably. "Hurry kills men. One tenet of my philosophy is that there is no pleasure quite so exquisite as minding other men's business. It is, you'll agree, no business of mine if an unfortunate gentleman elects to be done to death in a cabin on this ship. Yet it fascinates me. I pine to know the wherefore and the why. Do you know something?"

He shot the question at Matthew Kelton.

"What?" asked Kelton, deciding that he might as well be amused.

"In another incarnation I was a master detective. Sherlock Holmes and I are brothers under the skin. I thought it might help you if I brought my phenomenal powers of ratiocination to bear on this problem."

"I'll be glad of any help you can give me, Mr. Mond," said Matthew Kelton, and waited.

"Tell me all your theories," said Mr. Mond, "and I'll tell you where they're wrong."

"I'm afraid I must decline your kind invitation," said Matthew Kelton. "Suppose you tell me yours."

"I," said Mr. Mond, "am as full of theories as a banana skin is full of banana. First, I think it was that man who jumped into the sea."

"How do you know about him?"

"I heard the commotion on deck and came out to investigate. Doubtless in the excitement you did not notice me looking on, my elegant form disguised as a Shetland pony."

"No, I didn't see you," said Kelton. "Well, why do you think it was the sailor, Fest?"

"He has a brachycephalic head. Often a criminal stigma, Mr. Kelton. I know my Lombroso. Also my Maeterlinck."

"What has Maeterlinck to do with criminology?" asked Kelton.

"Not a thing," said Mr. Mond. "But we were talking about the colored sailor. I don't like his head, Mr. Kelton."

"That," said Matthew Kelton, thinking of Mr. Mond's own remarkable skull, "is hardly sufficient grounds for suspecting a man of a capital crime."

"Why did he leap into the ocean?" propounded Mr. Mond. "I heard some talk that he had seen the devil or some bogey-man with luminous eyes. Perhaps he did. But I know what the devil was."

"What?" asked Kelton; He was interested now.

In a solemn voice Mr. Mond made answer.

"His own conscience! That, sir, is the worst devil of all. Yes, sir. Fest killed that man Cleghorn—and was so pursued by the demon of his own conscience that he jumped into the sea."

"But why should Fest kill Cleghorn?"

"That," said Mr. Mond, "is a minor matter which I gladly leave to you to cope with."

"Thanks," said Matthew Kelton. Was this vast, peculiar man as imbecile as he sounded? Or was he a cunning man, playing the simpleton for some buried reason of his own?

"Theory Number Two," said Mr. Mond. "The doctor did it."

"Why do you say that?"

"His face is against him," declared Mr. Mond. "It has a sneaky look. Besides, who has the run of the ship? The doctor. Who could do a job like that, and think so little of it he could eat a hearty dinner soon after? The doctor. I don't like doctors, anyhow. They've persecuted me, the lying quacks. I'd like to twist their heads off—"

Mr. Mond's eyes shone and his big hands opened and closed as he said this.

"Not a very strong case, I'm afraid," said Matthew Kelton.

"I've another candidate for the honor," said Mr. Mond.

"Who?"

"The fellow who has the cabin next to mine."

"Who is that?"

"His name," said Mr. Mond, "is Varga."

"What about him?" Kelton did not need to simulate interest.

"He's an odd tomato, if ever there was one," said Mr. Mond. "In fact, I'm not sure he isn't twins."

"Twins?"

"Yes, sir. Follow this closely. He stays in his cabin. Goes there the minute he comes aboard, and hibernates, smoking cigarettes that smell like incense. My cabin reeks

with them. The smoke seeps through my ventilator. But
he isn't seasick; not he. I saw the steward leave his dinner
at his door, the whole works from olives to coffee,—why
even I would have had difficulty stowing such a meal away,
and I'm no mean eater. A bit later his tray is outside his
door, and he's polished off every plate. Pretty soon—this
is early in the evening—I hear him opening his door. I
open mine on a crack to get a look at him. He's a lanky
Johnny with a black Van Dyke—a sort of slick edition of
Svengali the hypnotist. He sneaks down the corridor—"

"And you followed him?" asked Kelton.

"Not me. He looked like the sort of chap who'd whip a
knife into your ribs without so much as 'by your leave.' If
he wanted to get the air, that was all right with me. Not
very much later he came back. I took another peek at him.
His door was open, perhaps an inch, and I could see into
his cabin. I could see his reflection, in the mirror over
his washstand—and may I be packed in oil and sold for a
sardine, Mr. Kelton, if he wasn't clean-shaven. Yes, sir. No
more beard than a cucumber. Then he shut his door tight
and bolted it. Now what do you think of that?"

"You're sure you saw a bearded man go out of the cabin,"
questioned Matthew Kelton, "and later, in the same cabin,
you saw a man without a beard?"

"Sure as I'm sitting here weighing two hundred and
sixty-nine pounds," said Mr. Mond. "Suppose I ask you a
riddle. What has two heads?"

"Give up," said Kelton.

"Two men," said Mr. Mond.

"You think, then, that there may be two men in Varga's
cabin?" interrogated Matthew Kelton.

"Looks that way, doesn't it?"

"Did you hear any voices in Varga's cabin? If two men
are in there, they'd do some talking, or at any rate some
whispering."

"Can't say I heard anything that sounded like conversation in there," Mond answered. "But that proves nothing. For one thing this old scow squeaks and rumbles so where I am that it would be hard to hear whispering. For another thing, Mr. Varga looks to be too knowing a cove to give the show away by chatting audibly with his partner. Why, Mr. Kelton, it would be the simplest thing in the world to smuggle another man aboard a boat like this. A man could amble aboard with the other visitors, and stay here. He'd need an accomplice, of course—some other passenger in whose cabin he could hide. The passenger could shoo the steward away, pretending he was sick and did not want to be disturbed. Once the ship landed in Bermuda, our stowaway friend could easily stroll off, for they're not very strict about landing cards down there."

"I'm obliged to you for this information, Mr. Mond," said Kelton, and meant it.

"Oh, I've got a lot more," said Mr. Mond.

"About Varga?" asked Matthew Kelton.

"No. Nothing more about him, except this: If that fellow isn't a wrong one I stand ready to eat, in any public place you care to mention, my brand new top hat, which I had made to order in London at a cost of six guineas. A fellow has no right to go round looking like a hypnotist—"

"Why do you say Varga looks like a hypnotist?"

"He's got such a nasty pair of eyes," answered Mr. Mond. "I didn't get much of a look at them, and, thanks be, they didn't get any sort of look at me, but I had a feeling that if he wanted to, Varga could stare at a man till he was woozy, and could then make him act like a trained seal."

"Indeed? You said you wanted to help in this investigation, Mr. Mond?"

"I did. I do."

"Very well. As far as you can, will you keep an eye on Mr. Varga? Try to discover if there really is another man in the cabin with him. But don't let him suspect you are watching him. Be discreet."

"I'll be discreet," promised Mr. Mond, "as a Boston matron in love with a professor of Greek."

Matthew Kelton consulted his watch and contended with a yawn, but Mr. Mond, lolling in his chair, ignored the hint.

"I'm rounding up quite a jolly corps of murderers," he remarked. "What a ship! I've never enjoyed myself so much on a trip. I'm thinking of commuting between New York and Bermuda on the dear old *Pendragon*. Such larks! Of course," Mr. Mond became extremely confidential, and said, with a knowing wink, "I see through this murder business. You can't fool an old trooper like me?"

His manner was so sure that Kelton forgot, for the moment, his fatigue.

"What do you mean?" he asked.

"Come now, Mr. Kelton," said Mond, "don't try to stuff me; I'm no olive. Why, the whole thing is a fake!"

"A fake?"

"Yes, sir. The captain is at the bottom of it. You see, he's not like these la-de-da transatlantic skippers who are really society men in uniform, full of palaver and chit-chat and social graces. He's just a bluff old sea-dog, with salt up his nose. The idea of having to carry passengers and answer a lot of questions from landlubbers and play the gracious host and all that gives him a swift, shooting pain. So what does he do? He gets you to spin a yarn about a corpse being found in one of the cabins. I expect you're a sort of social secretary in the pay of the line, going about getting up such entertainments. The passengers get all excited and entertain each other by jabbering about the awful happening. That leaves the captain in peace to drink his rum and run his ship. An interesting crime is better than a jazz-band any day—and less expensive. Why, there never was any Samuel P. Cleghorn, or any murder. It's all a sort of private moving picture—"

Matthew Kelton laughed.

"You're ingenious, Mr. Mond," he said, "but inaccurate. Unfortunately this is a very real and very grim business. If you'll come up to the ship's sick bay with me you can see for yourself that Cleghorn is, or rather was, an actual person, and that this murder was not in the least imaginary."

"I'll take your word for it," said Mr. Mond, hastily. "It was just a notion of mine. Not a bad one, either, I think. I'll try to sell it to one of the big steamship lines. Synthetic murders on shipboard; more entertaining than shuffleboard. Patented by T. Taylor Mond. There might be money in it, what?"

"Possibly," said Matthew Kelton, struggling with a yawn again.

"Now about this Mr. Westervelt," said Mr. Mond, and Kelton stopped yawning. "What about him?"

"Well, what about him, Mr. Mond?"

"There's a foxy clam for you!"

"How do you know?"

"I've talked with him," replied Mr. Mond. "Rather, I talked to him. I tried a little polite parlez-vous on him this afternoon, and again after dinner. It was like talking into a radio microphone. I'd say something, or ask something, and he'd let it lie. Honestly, I never encountered a man with so small a vocabulary and so stiff a tongue. I hate neat, secretive men. I'll bet my pearl studs against a bone collar button, when this affair is all washed up, you'll find that the cagey Mr. Westervelt has had a finger in it, somehow."

"How did you happen to talk with Mr. Westervelt after dinner?" inquired Matthew Kelton.

"Saw him up in the writing room, tucked away in a corner, doing cross-word puzzles in an old newspaper. I'd strayed up there to see if there might be a book I could read in what is humorously called 'the ship's library.' All I could find was a cookbook, 'French for the Trenches' and 'Little Women.' I took the cook book. Westervelt never gave me a tumble. There sat Westervelt, mum as a radish, sucking the point of his pencil and trying to think of a three-letter word for 'large Australian ostrich-like bird.' I greeted him and said something profound about the weather, and told him to try 'emu.' He wasn't rude, mind you. Didn't hand me the icy stare, or anything like that. Just sat there listening to me, and saying nothing beyond 'Yes,' 'No,' and 'Mumph.' The longest sentence I got out of him was when I asked him, point blank, his opinion about who committed the murder. He said, 'I have no opinion; I have no facts.' I finally gave up trying to get any conversation out of him, and read a chatty little piece in the cookbook about chicken livers *en brochette.*"

"Did he seem at all nervous?" asked Kelton.

"About as nervous as a cast-iron dog," said Mr. Mond. "At last he got up and went away. I'd sized him up as a small town optician or something like that, a worthy dullard, until I saw something which made me change my mind."

"What did you see?"

"As Westervelt passed me, saying good night as if it cost him two dollars a word to say it, his coat caught against one of the tables in the writing room, and for half a second the tail of it was held up. Mr. Kelton, he had something in his hip pocket which small town opticians do not carry—in one pocket a black jack, and in the other a mean looking revolver."

"You're sure it was a blackjack?"

"Certain. I was hit with one once. A footpad slugged me on Broadway one night. I bought the blackjack from him after the trial. Wanted it for a souvenir. Oh, yes, what

I saw in Westervelt's hip pocket was the handle of a black-jack."

"Very interesting. What do you make of it?"

"Perhaps," said Mr. Mond, lightly, "Westervelt is one of those high-powered salesmen you hear about. He's going down to Bermuda to sell lily bulbs to the natives, and he intends to make good in a big way, and he's taking some highly persuasive arguments in his hip pockets."

"By the way, Mr. Mond," said Matthew Kelton, "what happened to the blackjack you acquired?"

Mr. Mond looked amusedly at Kelton for a moment, then burst into his peculiar chuckle.

"What a forthright, straight-from-the-shoulder fellow you've turned out to be, Mr. Kelton," he said. "Well, I like you for it. I hate beaters-around-the-bush. I'll tell you. I have it with me, in my cabin. Since my experience with the bandit, I decided that if there was any slugging to be done, I might as well be prepared to do it. You see I go around a lot late at night, to night clubs and other places where the society is what Herr Baedecker calls 'mixed.' I don't mind being robbed by head waiters in a genteel way, but I have a prejudice against being knocked on the head by uncouth persons who care nothing about me personally but only want to lift my wallet. Do you want to see my little life preserver, Mr. Kelton?"

"No. Never mind, thanks."

Mr. Mond chuckled again.

"Now isn't this diverting?" he said. "The well-known finger of suspicion pointing my way! Think you can make out a case against me, Mr. Kelton? I hope not. I'd look ridiculous on a gallows."

"I have not said I suspect you, Mr. Mond," said. Matthew Kelton, seriously. "It is simply my practice to collect every scrap of information I can which might bear on the case in hand. The fact that you carry a dangerous weapon

is interesting, but not necessarily important. It's against
the law in New York, but that's your look-out. I quite
understand why you feel the need of protection after your
experience with the hold-up man. Also, let me assure you
that I have no wish to see you or any other innocent man
ornamenting a gibbet."

"My sentiments, exactly," said Mr. Mond. "I only wish
I'd been in my cabin this afternoon—about three—"

"Why?"

"I might have had some use for my blackjack."

"How so?"

"It isn't only a murderer who is disporting himself on
this ship! It's a thief as well."

"Were you robbed?"

"I was."

"What was taken?"

"I don't know—yet. I'm a careless sort in some ways.
Never know just what I have in my baggage. I've an h-drop-
ping valet in New York who stuffs a lot of things in my
bags when I go on a trip. I've a special bag for neckties.
They weren't touched, thank glory. But the rest of my kit
had a thorough going over. The fellow had no respect for
my pet shirts at all."

"You've missed nothing?"

"Oh, yes. There's a lady I know in Bermuda—an ex-
wife of mine—and I wanted to take her a little present.
I stepped into one of those upper Fifth Avenue dives and
let them soak me thirty-nine fifty for a dinky bottle of
perfume, the latest yelp from Paris they said, called *Amour
Est Notre Maître*. Well, Mr. Kelton, that bottle was in my
dressing-case because I put it there myself—and now it's
vanished, and I'm out thirty-nine fifty."

Kelton's brow crinkled.

"Mmmmmm," he said. "I'm glad you told me about
that. A singular thief, Mr. Mond."

"Probably he was scared away before he could get to my neckties," said Mr. Mond. "Well, I've one more contribution to make to the rogue's gallery."

He seemed, under his facetiousness, to be in earnest.

"Namely?" questioned Kelton.

"Mr. Kelton," said Mond, "has it struck you that there is one person of this ship neither of us has mentioned as being the possible murderer of Samuel P. Cleghorn?"

"You have gone over the list rather thoroughly," Kelton said.

"There is one person, though, I have not named," said Mr. Mond, unsmilingly. "That person had the opportunity to do the act. That person is clever, and strong enough to have done it. That person has shown an inordinate amount of interest in the case. That person has acted in a crafty way to smudge the trail leading to the real murderer—to avoid any suspicion of guilt. I accuse that person of the deliberate murder of Samuel P. Cleghorn."

"And that person is?"

"You, Mr. Matthew Kelton," said Mond.

Kelton's muscles tightened. He stared at the big man, who was regarding him fixedly. Then he said, quietly, "That's nonsense, Mr. Mond. I had nothing to do with Cleghorn's death and you can believe that or not, as you see fit. I grant that you are entitled to your suspicions, just as I am entitled to mine. If you feel that your suspicion of me amounts to a certainty, you are at liberty to tell it to Captain Galvin, and to ask my arrest and detention until I can be turned over to the authorities in Bermuda, for trial. I warn you, though, that with the flimsy evidence you have, you'd simply make even more of a laughing stock of yourself than nature has made you. Now, I'll bid you good night."

Matthew Kelton got up, went to the door, held it open.

"Now don't get shirty," said Mr. Mond, in an aggrieved tone. "I'm not going to do anything—yet. I'll have plenty of hard, cold, damning facts against you before this trip is over. I'm a sportsman—and I want to give you fair warning that I'm after you."

"I, too, am a sportsman, Mr. Mond," said Kelton, in a level voice, "and I want to warn you that I am after you, and that I, too, may be able to lay some hard, cold, damning facts before the authorities."

Mr. Mond, throwing back his huge head, laughed that chuckle of his, half bray, half cackle.

"Fair enough," he said. "It's a duel, then. You—or me. But listen, Kelton—suppose I did do it? Do you think I'd be so dumb as to bungle the job? Do you think I'd leave a waistcoat button in the dead man's hand or some such tyro stunt? You don't know T. Taylor Mond if you think that. No, sir if I committed this murder—I say 'if'—you'll never be able to prove it on me, smart as you are."

Mr. Mond lifted his bulk from the chair and strolled toward the door.

"Just for fun I'll tell you something, Kelton," he said. "I did do it. Now go ahead and try to prove I did. Good night."

With a bow and a mocking grin, Mr. Mond left the room. Kelton sank into a chair.

"Mad," he muttered. "Stark mad. And yet, is he? Where is the border line between madness and sanity, after all? Most murders are done by acute egomaniacs—Mond's type. They commit a crime with amazing skill and care, and then have to talk about it. Dr. Neil Cream, the London poisoner of half a dozen women, would never have been caught if he had not written anonymous letters to the police mentioning himself as a likely suspect. Is Mond such a madman? Or is he the other sort the police know so well—the man who always turns up in any celebrated case, who accuses himself of the crime when he wasn't within a hundred miles of the spot where it was committed? Was his challenge to me mere braggadocio? Simply a lunatic's desire to get some attention? In any event, Mr. Mond will bear watching. But not to-night. Merciful powers, I'm a tired man. Nothing short of shipwreck is going to get me out of this cabin again to-night."

He began, yawningly, to undress. He had slipped on his pajamas and was sleepily reaching for his tooth-brush, when he heard a sound—faint but distinct taps. They were not on his door. He listened. He thought he heard a door open, and voices, whispering. He cautiously opened his door. His own corridor was dark and quiet. The sounds must come from the next corridor, where there was but one stateroom, Cabin A, occupied by Miss Yate and her nurse. On bare, silent feet he stole along the corridor. He saw, heading for the stairs which led to the upper deck, two figures, their backs to him. One, unmistakably, was Captain Galvin. The other one wore a long dark cloak— and Kelton recognized the broad, short figure of the nurse, Julia Royd.

"Another conference," he said to himself. "Well, let them have it. It may mean a lot—or a little—or nothing— but I'm not going to try to find out tonight. I'm going to bed."

He did so. He was spent, mentally and physically. Deep sleep came to him a minute after he had switched out his cabin light.

10

VARGA

At seven, Matthew Kelton, habitually an early riser, awoke to find the morning sun flowing through his porthole. The second day at sea was bright and mild. The S.S. *Pendragon* had entered the gulf stream. Kelton dressed quickly. His rest had given him a new store of energy, and, he mused, as he slipped into his coat, he'd need all the energy at his command that day.

While dressing he endeavored to make some sort of halfway orderly summary of the facts in the case of the murder of Samuel P. Cleghorn. He shook his head in dire perplexity. Never had he been confronted by so inchoate, confused, contradictory a mass of facts, theories and guesses. The trails crisscrossed; they led up blind alleys. He thought of himself as a pack of hounds in a country teeming with foxes. But he was not discouraged. Mystery was the breath of life to him. He reaffirmed the resolution he had made to cut through that dense underbrush and penetrate to the heart of the matter—and to do it before the ship steamed into Hamilton harbor the next day.

He considered some of the more prominent facets of the case.

There was the confession of Russell Sangerson, to begin with. Sangerson had stated flatly that he had killed his uncle. Kelton was not satisfied with that confession.

A motive was present, but the story of the young man had been hazy on two important points—the time of the crime and the weapon employed. He had said that he had struck Cleghorn with a water carafe. Kelton examined the water carafe in his own cabin. It would be identical with the one in Cabin B. He picked it up, weighed it. It was an ordinary, plain glass bottle holding perhaps a quart and a half. Filled with water it made a heavy weapon, but, Kelton discovered, at the expense of a drenched sleeve, if you picked it up by the neck, and tried to swing it the water would pour out, for it had no stopper. Empty it was not very heavy. Not a very formidable weapon.

He went across to Cabin B, which had been locked after the removal of Cleghorn's body, but for which Kelton had been supplied a key by Captain Galvin. The cabin had been left, by his direction, in the state it was when the steward discovered the murdered man. Kelton went at once to the water carafe which stood in its wooden stand near the wash-basin. The carafe in Cabin B was, as he had expected, an exact duplicate of the one in his own cabin.

Kelton noted that it was full of water. He examined the neck for finger marks or other traces that the bottle had been grasped by a hand. He could find none. It was quite possible, of course, he reflected, that Sangerson, after beating Cleghorn to death with the carafe, had carefully refilled it with water, wiped off all finger marks with a towel, and put it back in its stand; and yet this was not likely. Sangerson, according to his own story, had struck his uncle in self-defense and in the heat of passion, and then had fled, panic-stricken. A man in that state, Kelton knew, does not become suddenly cool and calculating. He does not stop to obliterate finger marks. If he retains any presence of mind at all, he throws the weapon away—and there was a porthole convenient for that purpose. Kelton returned to his own cabin. He would subject Sangerson's story that he had used the carafe to a drastic and final test.

Taking his pigskin bag, Kelton stuffed one end of it with books, brushes and shoes so that it presented a hard, firm surface. Then he grasped his empty carafe by the neck, raised it, and brought it down violently on the end of his bag. At the third blow the body of the carafe was shattered. The indications had been that Cleghorn had been struck six or seven times at least. If Sangerson used the carafe, the chances were a thousand to one it would have broken. As it wasn't broken, or even cracked, Matthew Kelton's belief that Sangerson's confession was spurious seemed, to him, definitely established. Besides, Sangerson had not been at all sure of the time, for he had set it about half-past four, whereas Cleghorn had spoken to the steward, Larsen, a little after five, and the crime must have been committed some time between five ten and five forty. Sangerson, then did not do it. Why, then, had he, a young man seemingly in full possession of his reason, confessed to it?

Kelton thought of one reason immediately: because Sangerson knew who did do it, and was trying to protect the real murderer. That led to another question: for whom would a young man make so great a sacrifice? The obvious answer was: for someone he loved—and Sangerson loved Pauline Imlay. She, however, was clearly not guilty. Her own manufactured story about the golf clubs and the time was completely at variance with the facts. Kelton shook a baffled head, and considered another facet—the eyes.

What connection had those gleaming eyes with the crime? To whom did they belong? Was there, Kelton wondered, a sinister unknown on the ship, prowling about at night, in search of something, an unknown who was ready to take a human life, or a number of lives, to attain the object of his search?

Or was this unknown, if he existed, a maniac, who prowled and killed without a cogent reason? Mond?

This led Kelton to another line of thought. Someone on that ship was hunting for something. Kelton's own cabin had been ransacked. The baggage of the dead man had been gone through. A thief had visited the cabins of both Miss Imlay and Mr. Mond. He had taken from them only trivial loot—bottles of perfume. How explain that? The bottles had but slight intrinsic value. It would hardly be worth a thief's while to take the risk of being caught committing burglary for the sake of a few perfume bottles. An idea flashed across Kelton's mind. Suppose the unknown had reason to believe that in some bottle, in the possession of someone aboard the ship, was an object of great value—and he was determined to get that bottle and its contents? What would those contents be? The bottles were small. The only small objects of great value, Kelton reasoned, are jewels.

Forgetting that he was hungry, and that breakfast awaited him in the dining saloon, Matthew Kelton sketched a hasty outline in his mind of the sequence of happenings aboard the S.S. *Pendragon*. The Unknown learns that an object of great value is being transported to Bermuda by some passenger whose name he does not know. He embarks on the *Pendragon* intent on getting that object. Time is against him. He has only two days to attain his end.

The Unknown knows, or suspects, that the object is concealed in a bottle. So he starts at once to make a systematic search in the cabins of the other passengers. He starts with Cabin C. He is disappointed. Next he goes to Cleghorn's cabin. He is busily engaged in hunting through Cleghorn's baggage, when poor Cleghorn enters and catches him red-handed. The Unknown has not found what he is looking for and he realizes that Cleghorn will have him arrested as a common sneak-thief. From his point of view, there is only one thing to do, and he does it. On the mistaken theory that a dead man tells no tales, he murders Cleghorn, probably with a blackjack, or life-preserver, which such a man would be apt to carry. He continues his search. He is getting more desperate—and daring. He does find a bottle in Miss Imlay's room, but not the right one. He finds the door of Miss Yate's stateroom locked; so he swings down to take a look into her porthole, hoping doubtless that he can reach through and get the object, or at least locate it. He draws a blank there. The porthole is closed and Miss Yate is in her cabin. Perhaps he is afraid she may have recognized his face at the window. Anyhow, he conceals himself near the cabin of the three schoolteachers, awaiting an opportunity to burglarize other cabins. Miss Cobb, hurrying back from the writing room, comes upon him by chance in his hiding-place, and for an instant he loses his head. He is afraid she'll scream, or report his presence there; so he rushes out, and knocks her down and runs to a new place of concealment. He may even have intended to kill Miss Cobb, but his hurried blow went astray. Once again he ventures forth, this time to rifle the cabin of Mr. Mond. There he gets a bottle, but, as Mond said he had bought it recently and had not opened it, it is probably not the bottle the Unknown is after. Having gone this far in his search it is not likely that he will stop now. He'll try again. Where?

His encounter with the seaman, Fest, in the hold was probably an accident. The Unknown, probably to get away from one of the men patrolling the decks, slips into the first convenient hiding-place, which happens to be the bunk-room where Fest is lying. Fest, superstitious and cowardly, runs away, and the Unknown runs after him, perhaps to silence him with a blow on the head. Fest is so scared that he leaps or falls into the sea. Then the Unknown vanishes. Probably he did nothing more last night, or I'd have been notified of it. One other thing he probably did. While creeping about the deck, it occurred to him that it would be a good idea to put the wireless out of commission. In this way he doubtless hoped that no warning could be sent to the possessor of the desired object by somebody in New York or Bermuda, that the Unknown was aboard. He failed there because he was not aware of the existence of the auxiliary radio. Later, no doubt, he discovered that he had failed—and stole into the radio room to intercept any messages which might concern him. Why did he steal the messages directed to me? That wants explaining. A mistake, perhaps, on his part. A badly tangled business, surely.

"Well, anyhow," mused Kelton, when he had finished this narrative, "the story has a certain shape—it has a be-ginning, and a middle—but what about the end? There can be no end until I have made the Unknown a Known."

He went to the dining saloon for his breakfast. The captain was at the table, moodily finishing a breakfast which appeared to have consisted entirely of black coffee. Mr. Westervelt was there, too, freshly-shaven, trim, divid-ing his attention between a cross-word puzzle and some bacon and eggs. He nodded, politely enough, when Kelton wished him good morning, but had no comments to offer on the weather, the crime or anything else. The captain with a hasty "Nothing new to report" to Kelton, went out. The three schoolteachers, and Mr. and Mrs. Johnstone, the honeymooners, came to breakfast. The teachers seemed none the worse for their experience of the night before. The bright sunlight of the day had apparently restored their poise. Presently Mr. Mond appeared, with a loud, "Morning, everybody. Hope you slept well. I slept like a babe. Like a dozen babes, in fact."

He was an eye-compelling figure, for he had dressed for the tropics in baggy linen knickers, a blue and white striped flannel blazer, with a pith helmet like an inverted canoe. He bowed and smiled at Kelton, as if he had entirely forgotten their interview of the night before, and as he encompassed a prodigious breakfast, he entertained the others by describing the proper way to serve grilled clams on hot hickory ashes. Miss Imlay, Sangerson, Miss Yate and her nurse did not appear for breakfast; nor did Mr. Varga.

Matthew Kelton finished his breakfast quickly. As he ate he tried to plan his program for the day. What new events might take place, which might supply fresh trails for him to follow, he could not foresee, but there was one thing he decided he must do. That was to see Mr. Varga.

He went to Varga's cabin, and knocked. At first there was no answer. He knocked again. Then a curt, annoyed voice called out.

"Who is it?"

"Mr. Matthew Kelton."

"What do you want?"

"I'd like to have a talk with you, Mr. Varga—for a few minutes."

"I'm ill and can't see anyone," said the voice. It was a deep voice, cultivated, but with a faint trace of accent.

"It is important," said Matthew Kelton.

"I tell you I do not wish to be disturbed," said the voice petulantly.

"I'm sorry," said Matthew Kelton, firmly, "but this is a matter which cannot wait."

"Who are you, anyway?" demanded the voice in the cabin.

"I'm investigating the death of Samuel P. Cleghorn," answered Kelton. "You can refuse to see me, of course, but I think it would be unwise—"

Silence for a moment.

"Oh, is that what you want? Well, come in." The voice, surprisingly, had become almost pleasant. The bolt of the door was slid back and Matthew Kelton stepped into the cabin. The curtains were drawn and the cabin was dim. The air was heavy with tobacco smoke. Varga lay in his berth, wrapped in a black silk dressing-gown. It was difficult, in the faint light, to see his face clearly, but Kelton was aware of two things: a black, pointed beard and a pair of unusually brilliant eyes.

"I'm really not at all well," said Varga, "and strong light hurts my eyes. What is it that you want to see me about?"

Kelton's eyes had been surveying the cabin. It seemed to him impossible that anyone else could be concealed in it; there was no place where a full-sized man could hide.

"Mr. Varga," he said, slowly, "a terrible crime has been committed on this ship—"

"Yes, yes," put in Varga, impatiently. "The steward told me all about it. You think I know something about it, is that it?"

"I think it possible," said Matthew Kelton.

"What right have you to say that?"

The tall man in the berth did not ask it angrily; he spoke coolly, languidly.

"You are a passenger on this ship," said Kelton, "and it is not a large ship. I merely wish to get a statement from you of your movements since the ship sailed yesterday. I am getting similar statements from the other passengers."

Varga lit a fresh cigarette.

"Nothing easier," he said. "First of all, I know absolutely nothing about this crime beyond what the steward told me. I came aboard at the last moment, and went directly to my stateroom, and here I've stayed. I'm an invalid, and this trip is for my health. I've been out of my cabin but once—and that was yesterday between five and six—"

"Where were you then?" asked Kelton, quickly.

"Doing nothing more exciting than taking a hot salt bath in the bathroom at the end of the corridor," answered Varga. "Oh, you don't have to take my word for it. I see by your face that you are skeptical. Well, I can prove it. This is what I did: at five precisely I got into a tub of hot salt water, and there I stayed until a few minutes before six. A long salt bath is part of the treatment my physician prescribed for me. When I had finished my bath, I returned at once to my cabin and have been here ever since. Now—if you doubt my word—ask Castle, the steward. He unlocked the bathroom for me, and locked it after I left."

"You say that was the only time you were out of your cabin?"

"Yes."

"You did not go out later in the evening?"

Varga flipped away his cigarette and lit another one.

"No," he said.

"You weren't up on deck at all last night?"

"I was not."

"Near the radio room?"

"I told you," said Varga, "that I did not leave my cabin."

"I see. Well, Mr. Varga, thank you for your information. I hope the trip will improve your health."

Kelton, who had been sitting in a chair, stood up. As he did so his elbow brushed against the ash-tray, knocking it to the floor, and scattering its contents on the cabin rug.

"Sorry," he apologized. "Clumsy of me."

He bent over and began to sweep the ashes and stubs back into the tray.

"Never mind it," said Varga. "The steward will clean it up."

But Kelton insisted on picking up the stubs and replacing the ash-tray on the washstand near Varga's berth. Then with a "Good morning" he left.

The first thing he did was to hurry to a deserted corner of the deck. From his pocket he took the cigarette stub he had found outside the radio room, and compared it with the one he had deftly palmed while in Varga's cabin. A smothered exclamation came from him. They were both of the same expensive Egyptian brand. No doubt about it— the maker's name in small gold letters was printed around the cigarette just above the cork tip. That meant—what? That Varga had lied, had lied confidently, boldly. He was the man whose shadow Kelton had seen on deck. He was, probably, though not certainly, the man who had wrecked the radio and had dropped his cigarette. If he had lied about his excursion to the upper deck after dinner, had he also lied about how he had spent the time between five and six the day of the murder? Had he deliberately tried to set up an alibi?

Kelton sought out the steward who looked after Varga's cabin. He found him in a corner, just outside the bath-room, bent over a book—a detective story. Kelton knew his type—an undersized Londoner, with a pasty, vacuous, good-natured face, an obliging creature, and honest—too afraid of losing his job to be otherwise.

Kelton knew how to deal with that type. He approached him and spoke in the crisp voice of authority.

"Are you the steward in charge of these cabins?"

The steward put down his book and stood up, with a respectful bob of his head.

"Yes, sir."

"What's your name?"

"Bert Castle, sir."

"Been with the line long?"

"Seven years, sir."

"Like it here?"

"Haven't any complaint, sir."

"Married?"

"Yes, sir. Wife and two kids in Liverpool."

"Now, look here, Castle, I'm acting for the captain in a very important matter, and I'm going to ask you some questions. I want the right answers, understand?"

"Yes, sir." The steward fidgeted.

"I want you to tell me exactly when and where you saw Mr. Varga yesterday afternoon."

"'Im?" said the steward. "Well, sir, 'e tells me to drawr a 'ot hath for 'im at five sharp, and I done so. 'E goes into the bathroom and 'e's in there, lying in the tub till most six, soaking in the salt water, and reading a book."

"How do you know that?"

"'Cos I'm sitting right here all the time reading my book," answered the steward. "'E couldn't 'ave left the bathroom without my sceing 'im, sir. I'll take my hoath on that, sir."

"Did he return at once to his cabin?"

"'E did, sir. I went with 'im to bring 'im some fresh towels."

"Did he go out of his cabin later?"

"I wouldn't know that for certain, sir. I was off, 'aving my supper, part of the time. But I didn't see 'im leave the cabin, sir."

"Did Mr. Varga give you anything?"

The steward grinned.

"A tip, sir? Yes, sir. When 'e first came on 'e says to me, 'Hi'm a hinvalid,' 'e says, 'hand hi'm going to stay hin my cabin and may need a lot of hextra hattention, so 'ere's a ten spot for you, and hif you look after me proper there'll be another one for you when we reach 'Amilton,' he says."

"I see. Very open-handed, eh?"

"Yes, sir. Wish there were more gentlemen like 'im."

"Now, Castle, you are perfectly sure he was in the bathroom between five and six. Think before you answer. The truth is bound to come out, you know."

"'E was hin there, sir, between five and six, sir. I'm habsolutely sure. Hit's God's truth hi'm telling you, sir."

"Very well, Castle. That's all. Thank you."

"Hit ain't going to get me in hany trouble, sir?"

"No. Not if it's true."

"Hit's true, sir."

"Very well."

Matthew Kelton turned away. He wished that the steward was lying—but he felt almost certain that he was not. He examined the bathroom. It had only one door. If Castle was telling the truth, Varga had a strong, practically incontestable alibi.

Kelton went up to the promenade deck, to pace up and down, his head bent in thought.

"Good morning, Mr. Kelton," a voice greeted him. He looked up. It was Miss Esther Yate. She was sitting in a steamer chair, and at first he hardly knew her, she was so different from the night before.

11

Voices

"Good morning, Miss Yate."

Kelton stopped beside the steamer chair. He was amazed at the change in her. On the night before in her cabin, she had been wan, limp, highly nervous, a typical chronic invalid. Now she was a different woman. Her eyes were bright, and there was color in her face. Her manner was animated and spirited. Women, he knew, are supposed to look their worst in the glare of the sunlight, but it seemed to him that Miss Esther Yate looked very much better, as she sat there on the deck, than she had looked in the artificial light of her cabin.

"Sit down, Mr. Kelton," she said, "and tell me if you were able to discover the person who frightened me last night."

Matthew Kelton sat on the steamer chair next to hers.

"No," he said. "I didn't have much luck. Did he appear again?"

"I suppose," Miss Yate said, "it was silly of me to get into such a state of nerves about it. It was rather a shock, of course, but I shouldn't have taken on so."

"I don't blame you in the least," Matthew Kelton said. "Were you bothered again?"

"No. He may have appeared again. But, you see, once I've taken my sleeping-draught, nothing troubles me until morning. Sleep is a wonderful refuge from troubles, isn't it?"

"It's man's greatest escape from reality," agreed Matthew Kelton. He looked at her steadily. "Miss Yate," he said, "last night I said I had a feeling that your face was familiar to me. Now I feel sure of it. I hope you will not consider it impertinent if I ask you again a personal question?"

"Ask it," said Miss Yate, with a smile.

"Weren't you once on the stage—under the name of Esta Yale?"

She laughed.

"My secret is discovered," she said. "I might as well admit it. Yes, I was. But I gave up the stage—oh, years ago—and I prefer to be known under my real name."

"I remember seeing you in 'The Last Woman.' You were capital."

"Thank you, Mr. Kelton. There is still enough of the actress in me to enjoy a little flattery."

"A great many people were sorry when you gave up the stage," said Matthew Kelton.

"It's nice of you to say that," said Miss Yate. "I was rather sorry myself. But I found it the most trying, and overrated of all professions. There's hardly an actress who isn't dreaming of the day when she can retire to private life. And yet—well, there are very few of them, too, who don't come back to it—if they can. The stage virus is one which no inoculation seems to be able to cure. Anyone who has been connected with the theater—"

Her voice trailed off. The color left her cheeks. Julia Royd, the nurse, who had been standing nearby, apparently watching the sea, hurried to her side.

"I think you'd better go down to the cabin, now, Miss Yate. You've overtaxed your strength."

"Perhaps I'd better," said Esther Yate, feebly. Her head had fallen forward and she seemed about to faint. "Excuse me, Mr. Kelton."

Supporting her, with an arm around her shoulder, the nurse led her away. Kelton was left sitting there, wondering. One minute she was so animated, the next so frail and haggard. It seemed, almost, as if she were two persons.

Kelton tried to recall where he had seen a person behave like that before. Years before, he thought, he had had a somewhat similar, experience. Its details were not clear in his mind. He seemed to remember that he had been talking to a man in a café in Paris, and the man had been holding forth with great spirit on the art of Monet, when suddenly his voice died away, his whole body went flaccid, and he tottered away from the table. Fifteen minutes later the man returned and resumed the discussion with as much zest as he had shown before his collapse.

The case of Miss Yate resembled that one, Kelton thought. It interested him. He would ask Dr. Charlesworth for an opinion on it, he decided; then he remembered that he had no time to stray into the by-ways of curiosity just then. The ship was making good speed toward Bermuda— and the murderer of Samuel P. Cleghorn was still at large.

He turned his mind into another channel of thought. When Julia Royd, the nurse, had spoken, something had clicked in Kelton's mind. It was the voice of Julia Royd which gave him the idea. He had noticed her manner of speaking before, that broad, rather rough, accent. It struck him now that there was someone else on the ship who spoke with the same sort of accent—Captain Galvin. That accent, Kelton realized now, was the mark of a person born and brought up in Yorkshire. Royd—that was a Yorkshire name too, and Galvin might be—Kelton clapped his hand to his head. Here was something—merely a thread, perhaps, or a coincidence. Cleghorn came, originally, from Yorkshire, too. He had, according to Sangerson, spoken of "his boyhood in York." In his mind's eye Kelton sketched a triangle—Captain Galvin, Cleghorn, Miss Royd. Did the answer he was seeking lie, after all, within that triangle? If so, how could he get at it? Yorkshire folk are noted for being clannish and close-mouthed. If the captain and the nurse were guarding a secret, they could be depended upon to guard it well, stubbornly. It would be difficult to see the cards they held in their hands unless—he could force those hands. He remembered then the captain's badly concealed interest in young Sangerson. Were they all in it? What use could he make of Sangerson's confession—counterfeit though it might be?

He paused in his speculations. It exasperated him to remember how little that was concrete and certain he had to go on. Suppose the captain, the nurse, young Sangerson, were all mixed up in the case in some way? That did not square very well with his elaborate story of the Unknown, seeking a treasure.

Nor did it take into account the challenge of Mr. Mond. Farther down the deck he could see that gentleman's large and gaudy figure, as he sat near the three schoolteachers, giving free rein to his garrulity and punctuating his anecdotes with resounding chuckles. If his admission that he had brought about the death of Samuel P. Cleghorn were true, then he was a singularly light-hearted murderer, Kelton thought. Could it be true? Mr. Mond was big enough, probably strong enough to have done it—but a motive was lacking, so far as Kelton could see. It was difficult for Kelton to see any connection between Cleghorn, a hard-headed, dour businessman who led a rather arid and secluded life and Mond, idler, globe-trotter, habitué of night clubs, who lived the life of an obese social butterfly.

Yet it was not impossible that their paths had crossed. Kelton's first impulse had been to discount Mond's words of the night before, to ascribe them to an aberration on Mond's part, or to a perverted sense of humor. True or not, they complicated the issue.

"If one more person confesses the murder of Cleghorn," said Kelton to himself, "I'll feel like sinking the boat. My head is spinning. I'm like a chicken in a field of crickets—everywhere I turn I see a self-confessed murderer. Well, no good comes out of fretting. There must be an answer—the one, right answer."

Pondering over what place to assign to Mr. Mond in the crazy-quilt picture, he made his way toward the cabin of Dr. Charlesworth.

On his way he passed a figure, wrapped in a blanket, a cap pulled down over his eyes, apparently asleep in a steamer-chair. It was Mr. Westervelt. As Kelton passed him, from the corner of an eye he noted that Mr. Westervelt was not asleep at all, but was watching him intently. Kelton stopped.

"Pleasant day, Mr. Westervelt," he said.

"Yes."

"Is this your first trip to Bermuda?"

"Yes."

"Staying long?"

"No."

"That's a sad affair—the death of Mr. Cleghorn," remarked Kelton.

Mr. Westervelt regarded him from expressionless eyes. After a long silence, he said, "All crimes are sad affairs."

"What do you think about it?"

Mr. Westervelt was silent again, then he used the words he had used to Mr. Mond the night before.

"I have no opinion; I have no facts."

"A sensible view to take," agreed Kelton, wondering how he could break through the other man's reserve. He tried again.

"Going to Bermuda on business, Mr. Westervelt?"

"Yes."

"How are business conditions down there now?"

"I don't know."

Matthew Kelton was nettled.

"You know I'm investigating this case," he said.

"Yes."

"As a matter of course I'm getting statements from all the passengers about their movements yesterday. I'd like one from you, Mr. Westervelt."

The man did not answer at once. Then he said, with no show of emotion, "You shall have one. I spent the afternoon on deck, right in this chair, doing cross-word puzzles, and dozing. I went down to my cabin to wash up at six-twenty."

His manner became a shade less impersonal.

"Mr. Kelton," he said, "I realize that my unsupported word may not be enough to convince you that what I've said is true. In your place, I'd want a lot stronger alibi than that. However, the fact is, it is true—as you will learn. It will be wise, and it will save you time, if you will accept my assurance that I had nothing at all to do with the murder, and that I know nothing about it that will help you. To-morrow I think I can convince you of that. Now I am not in a position to do so."

Toward the end he was speaking with great earnestness.

"Thank you," said Matthew Kelton, and continued on his way. He was impressed by the ring of sincerity in the man's words. Sincerity, he reflected, can, of course, be simulated. He was puzzled by what Westervelt had said. Why could he convince Kelton of his innocence to-morrow, and not then and there?

"Well, anyhow," decided Kelton, "I can hold him to his promise to-morrow. Before he sets foot off this ship, he'll have to make good his words. Either he's telling the truth, or trying to get away with a brazen bluff. That is at least one question I can leave to time to answer. I'll put the reticent Mr. Westervelt in a pigeonhole and leave him there for the time being."

He found Dr. Charlesworth in his cabin, which was also his office. Kelton had two motives in going to see the doctor. He wanted an opportunity to study him at close range. A man's personality, a word he chanced to drop, a gesture—these in other cases in the past had given Matthew Kelton valuable hints. He wanted, also, to consult the doctor's medical library, if he had one, which Kelton considered unlikely. He had already catalogued Dr. Charlesworth as a man going nowhere in particular, and as one who probably did not exert himself to keep up with the latest movements and discoveries in his profession.

Dr. Charlesworth greeted him courteously.

"Not a patient, I hope?" he said.

"No," answered Kelton, with a smile. "I'm much too busy to be seasick. My trouble is mental! My mind is full of pugnacious facts, all fighting with each other. Can you help me?"

"Not much, I'm afraid," said the doctor, motioning Kelton to a seat. "My practice on this ship is confined to giving out big brown pills and to painting with iodine ankles sprained by people hurrying out of the dining room. The only mental purge I know is psychoanalysis—and that takes time."

As he talked, Kelton was looking over the cabin. He had half-way expected it to be slipshod, and in disorder. It was, in fact, meticulously neat and orderly. Cases against the walls were filled with books, thick, scientific-looking tomes. Kelton ran his eyes over the titles and was again surprised. He knew enough about medical literature to see that the doctor's library was unusually complete and up-to-date.

"That's only part of my library," the doctor remarked. "I've a lot more books in a storeroom. I've a hard time keeping my books. Passengers are always dropping in for a pill, and trying to pinch one of my books. I suppose they hope they are naughty. I've finally worked out a scheme. I gently take the medical book away from them and loan them a copy of J. K. Huysmans' 'Against the Grain.' That has enough psychopathology in it for any layman."

Kelton laughed.

"A remarkable book," he said. "What men will do to find new sensations—" He stopped. Another idea had clicked in his mind.

"Doctor," he said, "what do you think about this murder?"

"I haven't the information you must have about it, Mr. Kelton," answered the doctor. "I'm hardly in a position to have any definite theory. I'm not much of a psychologist, or detective, you see. My field is the physiology and chemistry of metabolism. That's why I'm on this ship. This job gives me leisure for study and research. I'm sorry, but I'm afraid I can't shed much light on the mystery."

"You've no theory at all?"

"No. I have only the medical evidence to go by. To tell the truth I've been so engrossed in a new book on vitamins I haven't thought much about the matter. All I know is that Cleghorn was beaten to death by a series of powerful blows which crushed his skull, blows delivered by a heavy instrument, in the hands of a person of more than ordinary strength. Who did it, or why it was done, I haven't the faintest notion."

"How long had he been dead?"

The doctor smiled.

"I'm not one of those wizard doctors of detective fiction who can fix the time of a man's death within ten seconds by glancing at his brow," he said. "In Cleghorn's case *rigor mortis* had set in—but it is a gradual process, you see. It begins usually within an hour or two after a man's death—but there are cases on record where it has started within fifteen minutes after life has become extinct; also there are other cases where *rigor mortis* was not observable for several hours, due to conditions of temperature. Naturally heat delays the process. So, you see, the man in Cabin B might have been dead twenty minutes, or several hours. Your guess is as good as mine."

"Thank you, Doctor. Now let me ask you something more. It may not be exactly in your field, but could you give me any idea what ailment Miss Esther Yate is suffering from?"

"Oh, the lady in the invalid chair," said Dr. Charlesworth. "No, I can't tell you much about her. She hasn't required my professional services. I've seen her, of course, and I'll admit I've taken more than a passing interest in her case. I've had a brief chat with her, about things in general—flying fish and porpoises mostly—, but I'm not enough of a diagnostician to hazard an opinion without a very thorough examination. I had a feeling, though, that she is not suffering from any ordinary complaint."

"Really? Doctor, do you think it possible that she is a drug-addict?"

The doctor considered a moment.

"Possible, yes. I'll admit I asked myself that question. I had considerable experience with poor devils suffering from various forms of the drug habit before I gave up private practice. I got rather expert in spotting them, and classifying them. Probably you know that users of any of the commonly used drugs, such as morphine, cocaine, opium, hasheesh, ether and so forth, show the particular signs of the particular drugs. I won't go into that now, but a specialist can tell a user of opium from a user of cocaine without much difficulty. Now my offhand impression of Miss Yate was that she uses or has used drugs in some form—but in what form I'm not prepared to say. None of the ordinary signs which point to one drug or another are present. And remember this, Mr. Kelton, though it is dangerous for a doctor to admit he may be wrong, I'll admit to you that my suspicion about Miss Yate may be entirely without basis. Her trouble may be psychic—and any honest doctor will admit that in the realm of the mind the best he can do is grope and hope."

"Can you tell me anything about Mr. Mond?" was Matthew Kelton's next question.

"There again I can only guess," answered the doctor. "He's not completely normal, I'm fairly sure of that. I've had a visit from him."

"You have? Tell me about it."

"He came to me this morning to get a pill for indigestion," said the doctor, "and, after seeing him eat, I wondered he didn't need a stick of dynamite. His behavior was strange. He took the pill, tossed it into the air, and caught it as it fell in his open mouth. Then he drank six glasses of water. Then he said he felt like singing and asked me if I wouldn't join him in a duet. When I declined, he sang 'Life on the Ocean Wave'—and stopped in the middle to ask me which I considered most painful, hanging, electrocution or shooting. I'm interested in nuts; so I talked to him. He's very much down on doctors, it seems. Got really rabid about it. I questioned him and found that he had once been in Dr. Morgenstern's Sanitarium where they treat rich alcoholics and mental nervous cases. His particular kick was that Dr. Morgenstern had discharged him and had written on his report, 'Harmless.' Mond seemed to resent that a lot. 'I'll show him who's harmless,' he said, a number of times."

"Do you think he is harmless?" questioned Kelton.

"Yes, I do," answered Dr. Charlesworth. "I know Dr. Morgenstern and his work. He's about the best alienist in America—and if he pronounces Mond harmless, the chances are a thousand to one he is right."

"But there's one chance in a thousand he's wrong?" asked Kelton.

"I suppose so. No doctor is infallible. Still, I think he's right in Mond's case. The fellow struck me as being a super-egoist, the sort of chap who has to have the spotlight trained on him, and who seeks to attract attention by his clothes, his talk and his behavior. It's an infantile, a show-off type. Mond is really a great big baby and should be treated as such. I'll bet if you threatened to spank him he'd begin to blubber."

"Thanks for the suggestion," said Matthew Kelton. "It may prove very useful."

"I'd like to have the moving picture rights to the scene when you spank Mond," said the doctor.

"It will be a metaphorical spanking, I think," said Kelton.

"Do you think he had anything to do with the murder?"

"He may have."

The doctor shook his head.

"I doubt it," he said. "I doubt it very much. He has a too well-developed example of what Dr. Stekel calls 'the beloved ego' to do anything which might cause him real pain."

"That's very illuminating, Doctor," Matthew Kelton said, "and I'm much obliged to you. I wonder, now, if you'd let me consult some of your books. An idea, so tenuous that I hate to put it into words, came to me just now. I'm not going to explain it—yet. I'll have to do a good bit of research first."

"My library is at your disposal, Mr. Kelton. So am I," said Dr. Charlesworth.

"Thank you. Is that book 'Against the Grain' here?"

"Yes, on that second shelf. Do you expect it to help you?"

"It has given me an idea," Kelton replied. "It is many years since I read it, but I remember vividly the decadent young man who is its hero. I recall how he was satiated with all the usual worldly sensations, so he set out to discover new thrills for himself. He devised strange new vices. It is one of those vices which particularly interest me just now."

"Can I help you, Mr. Kelton?"

"No, thank you, Dr. Charlesworth. I hope to be able to work this out by myself."

"Very well. I'll take a turn on deck. Please make yourself at home here."

Matthew Kelton plunged at once into his reading. So absorbed was he that he did not notice the passage of time, nor heed the luncheon gong. When he finally glanced at his watch, an annoyed exclamation escaped him.

"The whole morning gone and nothing tangible done— except a probable wild-goose chase launched." He put down the book.

He hurried to the dining room. It was empty. The others had finished their lunch. The dining room steward was obliging, however, and Matthew Kelton was supplied with a chop and a salad. He did not know he was eating a chop and salad. His mind was so intent on the problem that he hardly knew he was eating at all.

Just as he finished his lunch, Captain Galvin entered the dining room. The day had brought no peace to the captain. He seemed distraught, and he seemed, too, to be trying to conceal the fact. He hurried to Kelton.

"Ah, Mr. Kelton," he said, "Here you are. I've been looking for you."

"Some new development, Captain?"

"Yes," said the captain, hoarsely, "the eyes have been seen again."

12

WHO DID IT?

"The eyes!" cried Kelton. "Where?"

"Down below—near the galley," answered Captain Galvin. "Mr. Kelton, I'm not a religious man—but this newest occurrence comes pretty near convincing me that there is a devil."

"Why? What did he do?"

"He killed Caesar."

"One of the crew?"

"Not exactly. Caesar was a dog. We almost considered him one of the crew, though. He'd been on this ship eight years. He was a great pet. If I get my hands on the man who killed him, God help him. As for the crew, they talk of lynching him. They loved Caesar."

"Give me the facts," said Kelton.

"Caesar," said Captain Galvin, "was an English bull-dog, the biggest I ever saw, and a grand scrapper. With people he knew—and of course he knew all the officers and crew—he was gentle, but let a stranger come near him, alone, and there was bound to be trouble. He was kept down in the crew's quarters, because we didn't want him chewing up any of the passengers. I saw Caesar go for a fellow once when we were anchored at the pier in Hamilton—a sneak-thief the man was—and Caesar nearly killed the man before we pried them apart. I'm telling you this because it has a bearing on what happened just now. No, that dog wasn't a coward. Now, listen to this."

"I'm listening," said Kelton.

"The men, to amuse themselves, used to play a little game with Caesar. Outside the galley is a long narrow passageway—just wide enough for one man—leading to a door which connects with the engine room. The men used to stand in the galley and throw a ball down the passageway. Caesar would run after it and retrieve it, but before he could get back to the galley they'd close the galley door leaving Caesar in the dark. He would bang and scratch at the door till it was opened. Not much of a sport, you'll say, but on shipboard men will do anything to pass the time. It was this game which cost Caesar his life."

"How?"

"George Harris, the cook, was in the galley and Caesar was playing around, when suddenly Caesar began to bristle, the way he always did when he sensed that a stranger was around. Usually, soon after he began to bristle, he went for the stranger—but not this time. He cowered close to George. He whimpered. He showed, in short, in every way that an animal can, that he was afraid. George couldn't understand it. He'd never seen the dog behave that way before. He got out the ball and made a motion to toss it down the passageway. Caesar actually clung to his arm, as if he wanted to prevent him from throwing the ball. George remembered all this, of course, afterward, when it was too late. Finally, he did throw the ball, and said "Go get it, Caesar!" Caesar hung back. He'd never refused to obey that command before. George thought the dog was playing, and pushed him out in the corridor. Caesar started to walk, very slowly, down the passageway, his hair standing on end. George, according to custom, shut the galley door. Then he heard Caesar growl, then there was a scuffling noise, and the poor dog let out a sharp cry of pain which was broken off short. George flung open the galley door. He swears he saw the face of someone standing in the door at the other end of the passageway—the face of someone very tall, with blazing eyes. Then, like a flash, the face disappeared. George ran down the corridor, and there lay Caesar. His body was twitching, but before George could get him back into the galley he was dead. Mr. Kelton, that devil had broken Caesar's neck—as cleanly as you could break that stalk of celery with your fingers!"

"How horrible!" exclaimed Kelton. "Poor dog, he sprang at the stranger, I suppose, and paid for his courage with his life. What have you done, Captain?"

"I've turned out the entire crew and had the men make a thorough search of the ship below deck. I should have done that early this morning but I couldn't spare the men."

"What did they find?"

"Nothing—absolutely nothing. Not even a trace."

"I'll go below with you, Captain," Kelton said. "I want to examine the scene."

Together they went to the passage-way leading to the galley where Caesar had met his fate. A light was brought and Kelton, on hands and knees, examined the floor.

"No sign of footprints," he muttered. "But, then, there wouldn't be on shipboard—no dusty or muddy feet. What's this?"

He picked up something which looked like a flake of isinglass, about the size of a postage stamp, but oval in shape. He examined it closely, and shook his head.

"Where do you keep your provisions?" he asked of Harris, the cook.

"Perishable stuff is kept in the big ice-box the other side of the galley," Harris answered. "Fish, meat, eggs and so forth."

"Are the provisions brought in through this passage-way?"

"Yes, sir. Most of them."

"I see," said Kelton, disappointedly. "Now I'll take a look at the dog."

Caesar had been a magnificent animal, with bowed legs and a potent-looking undershot jaw. His head was jerked back in an unnatural position as he lay on the galley floor. Captain Galvin was right. The dog's neck was broken. Kelton bent over the dead animal.

"It wasn't done with a blow," he said. "In that case it's likely the head would be bent forward. The head is bent back. That looks as if Caesar was not struck with some weapon, but was caught, and his neck snapped. It would take terrific strength to do that."

He examined the dog's mouth.

"I think," he said, "Caesar got in one bite before he was killed. Look—there's a trace of blood on his fangs—and—what's this?"

Adhering to one of the dog's lips was a small micalike object, flat and translucent—in size, shape and composition identical with the thing Kelton had picked up in the passageway.

"I'm going back to my cabin," he announced. "I've an idea—a crazy idea—and I'm going to try to develop it. Tell your men to be on their guard, Captain Galvin. We have a cruel and malevolent enemy of mankind to contend with."

On his way to his cabin, Kelton stopped at the radio room and dispatched two messages. One was to B. Hong, Mott Street, New York. The other was to Professor Adrian Tyne, Silvermine, Connecticut. The one to Mr. Hong was in code.

He started for his cabin, via the promenade deck. Mr. Westervelt was in his chair, looking as if he were asleep, although he wasn't. The honeymooners, Mr. and Mrs. Johnstone, were sitting in steamer chairs, very close together, slyly holding hands. The three schoolteachers were reading books about the flora of Bermuda. Kelton hurried along the deck. A voice stopped him.

"Good afternoon, Mr. Kelton."

It was Miss Esther Yate, in her steamer chair, and once again Kelton was astonished by the change in her. He had seen her led to her cabin by her nurse, very weak, very pale. Now she had color in her face, and she was talking, with a great deal of energy, to Mr. Mond. Her manner was that of a person who is physically on the crest of the wave. Mr. Mond, obviously, was captivated—so much so that he was listening, and was not, according to his habit, monopolizing the conversation.

"Good afternoon, Miss Yate," said Kelton. "Feeling better?"

"Much, thank you. How is your investigation getting on?"

Kelton was visited with an inspiration.

"It is practically completed," he answered, looking not at her, but at Mr. Mond. "I haven't a cruel nature, Miss Yate, but I'll admit I'll take a certain satisfaction in seeing the man hung."

He addressed Mr. Mond.

"Mr. Mond," he said, very gravely, "I'd like to have a few moments conversation with you in my cabin, please."

"Why? What's up?" asked Mr. Mond, looking startled.

"I'll tell you, if you'll come with me," said Mr. Kelton.

"But I'm enjoying Miss Yate's society so much," protested Mr. Mond.

"I regret to have to deprive you of it," said Kelton, "but I feel sure she'll excuse you. This is an urgent matter, Mr. Mond, and a most serious one for you."

"I'll come," said Mr. Mond, rising, his large face troubled. "Excuse me, Miss Yate."

"Yes. Will you be back?"

"Very soon, I hope."

Mr. Mond followed Kelton down to the latter's cabin.

In his most solemn manner, Matthew Kelton closed the door, locked it, and waved Mr. Mond to a seat. Then for a long time Kelton sat staring fixedly at Mr. Mond, and saying nothing.

Mond stood the tension as long as he could, and then burst out, "Look here, Kelton. What do you want of me?"

In a sepulchral voice, Matthew Kelton said, "Mr. Mond, last night you made an admission and issued a challenge. I am prepared to act on that challenge now. I have asked Captain Galvin to arrest you, and confine you in the ship's brig for the murder of Samuel P. Cleghorn. You will be delivered either to the police in Bermuda, or the police in New York. In Bermuda, I believe, the penalty for murder is hanging. In New York, it is electrocution. I do not know enough about the law of the sea to know which will be your fate—but you can be sure it will be one or the other—"

During the recital Mr. Mond underwent a very palpable change. His round face grew pale, his lips began to quiver. Suddenly he broke into sobs, the sobs of a child caught with his fingers in a forbidden jam pot.

"Now, Mr. Kelton," he cried, "don't do that. Please don't do that. I didn't do it, honest I didn't. I was just fooling. Can't you take a joke?"

"This is no joke," said Matthew Kelton.

"It was, I swear it was," wailed Mr. Mond. "I never killed anybody. Why, I couldn't harm a kitten, honest I couldn't. I was just talking, that's all. I thought it would be sort of exciting to have you think for a while that I was a murderer and trail me around and get all the others watching me. I never thought you'd take my confession seriously, honest I didn't. Nearly all afternoon I was talking to the purser—and he'll bear me out, I know he will. You're not going to get me hung, are you, Mr. Kelton?"

Mr. Mond's fright and penitence bore every evidence of being genuine.

"Mond," said Matthew Kelton, severely, "I'm going to accept your explanation. I'm not going to take action against you. I have not asked the captain to arrest you, nor do I intend to. I'm going to give you a piece of advice: curb your sense of humor or your sense of self-importance. A confession of murder is a very sorry jest. One of these days someone less tolerant than I am will take you seriously and you'll find yourself in jail, which is not pleasant, or dancing at the end of a rope, which is even less so. That's all."

Kelton's words had restored to Mr. Mond a faint trace of his old swagger.

"I guess you're right," he said. "I've acted like a fool. You won't tell anybody about this, will you?"

"No," promised Kelton. "It won't be necessary. Now please get along out of here. You've caused me to waste a lot of time and thought."

"I'm sorry for that, Mr. Kelton," said Mr. Mond, and took his departure, looking like a caricature of a chastised schoolboy.

Kelton's face relaxed into a smile.

"That gets the joker out of the deck," he remarked. "Lucky thing I called on the doctor, and read a few case histories in his books. The big, soft sap! The half-baked nuisance! Well, anyhow, that's one confession accounted for. Now—what about the others?"

For the first time since the start of the case, Matthew Kelton had an uninterrupted period when he could concentrate. He had made a wager with himself—a new and very expensive microscope—that he'd get to the bottom of the mystery before the ship's side scraped the Hamilton wharf the next day. As he sat there in his cabin, it seemed to him that the chances were heavily against his winning

his bet. Mond was eliminated. But there remained Sangerson, the captain, Westervelt, Varga—and Miss Royd. All
possibilities. Yet his case against any one of them was very
far from being strong. He had surmises, conjectures, theories—and they added up to—what? Confusion.

He wished the answers to his radiograms would come
in. He needed all the rays of light he could get, no matter
how puny they might be. He focused his mind on the incident of the dog's death.

On the surface, it seemed to be easy to explain. The
dog had detected the presence of the stranger. With an
animal's intuition where danger is concerned, he had been
afraid of the stranger. Then, with the courage of his breed,
he had attacked—and been killed. His killer had fled and
concealed himself. Where? The captain had said the crew
had made a thorough search—but sailors, in general, are
not notable for their intelligence, and it was probable they
had been outwitted.

Kelton examined again the particles, like bits of isinglass, he had collected in the passageway and from the
mouth of the dead dog. He examined, too, one of the first
things he had collected—the tuft of hair he had found
caught in the washstand in Cabin B. The hair was long,
coarse, rather brittle. Kelton clapped his hand to his fore-
head, an outward sign that something was stirring briskly
within.

Was this another such case as Poe described in his ma-
cabre story "The Murders in the Rue Morgue"? There the
killer had been a gorilla. That tuft of hair was not from a
human head; it was from some animal. What was a gorilla's
coat like? Kelton tried to remember. Shaggy, certainly. But
was it brindled, as these hairs were? Then he laughed at
himself for getting so excited by such a fantastic idea. A
gorilla is larger than most men. He is smart enough in his
native African jungle, but on shipboard, wasn't it probable

that he'd be completely bewildered, and would be sure to be seen?

Besides, how account for the presence of such an animal on the S. S. *Pendragon*. Gorillas do not drop from the sky, nor emerge from the sea. Their habitat is Africa—and a small section of Africa, at that. There are very few of them in captivity, Kelton knew. No, the gorilla theory was absurd. He'd have to seek a less fantastic explanation.

All afternoon Kelton sat in his cabin—thinking, thinking. He found some answers to his questions, but they were cancelled by other answers. The dinner gong broke in on his speculations. He ate his dinner in silence. Mr. and Mrs. Johnstone were present, and the three schoolteachers, the purser and the doctor. Mond was there, in a very subdued mood, which did not, however, interfere with his consumption of pounds of mashed potatoes and quarts of ice-water. Mr. Westervelt also appeared at dinner, as discreet, correct and self-contained as ever. The captain, Miss Imlay, Sangerson, and Varga did not come to the table, nor did Miss Yate and her nurse.

The net result of all Matthew Kelton's cogitation that afternoon had been a decision to try another of his "psychological depth-bombs." He had made up his mind to explode it—after dinner—and he had fixed for the scene of the explosion the cabin of Captain Galvin.

He found the captain in. The captain was puffing at an old briar pipe, but was getting little solace from it, to judge from his face. He looked very tired.

"Good evening, Mr. Kelton," he said, trying his best to appear genial and at his ease. "Any luck?"

"Yes," said Matthew Kelton. "If you want to call it that. It's a mighty unpleasant duty you wished on me, Captain. It's the sort of duty which makes me feel rather unfriendly to that abstract thing we call justice. I hate to be the instrument of a justice which will cause people who are not really criminals to suffer for a single lapse from the right path."

"I don't follow you, Mr. Kelton," said the captain, but his manner showed that he had more than an inkling of what was coming. "Have you caught your man?"

"I have," replied Matthew Kelton. "I have come to you to ask you to place him under arrest."

"Who is he?" The captain's voice trembled.

"Russell Sangerson."

"But what have you against him?"

"Enough. Motive. He was the nephew and heir of the dead man. They quarreled. Sangerson struck him down."

"But that is simply a guess—"

"It is not a guess, Captain," said Matthew Kelton. "Sangerson has confessed."

"What?"

"I repeat," said Kelton. "Russell Sangerson has confessed to me that he killed his uncle, Samuel P. Cleghorn. I have sought in vain for other explanations of the murder, but have found none. I am sorry for young Sangerson but I see only one course open. Arrest him and turn him over to the detective who is aboard the *Tarragonno.*"

The captain said nothing. Then, finally he spoke, and his voice was thick, and his face set.

"I'm not going to arrest Sangerson," he said.

"You refuse? Why?" Kelton shot at him.

"Because," answered Captain Galvin, "he's not guilty of the murder—and I know who is."

13

STRONGER THAN DEATH

"You know who is guilty?" gasped Kelton.

"I do," said the captain. "I know."

"Who?"

The captain seemed more composed.

"There's a story that goes with it," the captain said. "I want you to listen to the story before I tell you the name. I'm not much at stories—but I'll do my best. We've plenty of time—now that your hunt is over. Here, try this cigar, Mr. Kelton."

Kelton lit the cigar, and leaned back in his chair. The cabin's light was on the captain's weather-beaten face. The captain put down his pipe, which had gone out, and sighed.

"The story begins," he said, "in a little Yorkshire village; Abbott's Glade, its name is, a tiny market town where the nearby countrymen come to sell their produce. It begins some thirty years ago. Were you ever in Yorkshire, Mr. Kelton?"

"Once," replied Matthew Kelton. "I stopped off in York for a day to see the cathedral."

"Then you hardly know Yorkshire and its people, Mr. Kelton, and this is a story about those people," the captain said. "Yorkshire people are not easy to know. A stranger could spend a good many years among them without really

understanding them at all. He wouldn't like them much—
at first. They might seem hard—sullen, you might say.
They don't talk much, but they work hard. They're farming folk, mostly, living close to the soil, and they're not
rich. They're thrifty with what little money they make,
because they have to be. People from London call them
rough, uncouth; they don't see beneath the surface and see
that under the roughness are characters as rugged and solid as the Yorkshire hills. They're a simple, strong people,
Mr. Kelton—and they love that way, aye, and hate that
way too. There's an old saying in Yorkshire—a riddle, you
might call it—What is stronger than death? The answer is:
Love. You'll not hear of many divorces among the real people of Yorkshire. When a man is 'for' a woman, as they say
there, he is for her always. When a Yorkshire man gets to
know you, and you're honest with him, and he likes you,
you have a friend for life, a friend who'll burn off his right
hand for you. And, it's true, too, if you wrong a Yorkshire
man, you've made a bad, black enemy, who will not forget,
but will bide his time and pay you back, if he has to follow
you to hell to do it."

The captain lit his pipe again.

"I'm a Yorkshire man," he said, "born and reared in
Abbott's Glade, on my father's little farm. There have
been Galvins in that part of Yorkshire—near the Scotch
border—for many a century. I had four brothers and five
sisters, and my father was a poor man, bent with work. It
was a sort of family tradition that one of the younger sons
should follow the sea—there was a Galvin with Nelson
at Trafalgar— and it was decided, when I was just a lad,
that I was to be a sailor. I was glad. I've always loved a
seafaring life. So I put a pine chest full of my clothes on
my shoulder, and went off to be a cabin boy in the merchant marine. I liked the life; I'd been strictly brought
up; so I paid attention to my duty and began to rise in

the service, and I looked forward to the day when I'd have a ship of my own to command. I'd just turned nineteen, and was making good wages—and saving them—when I got shore leave and went to stay a month with my parents in Abbott's Glade. I hadn't been back home in three years, for my ship had been off in the China Sea. Well, a lot can happen in three years—particularly to young people. The first evening I was home I strolled over to the next farm to spin the people there a few yarns about my adventures in foreign parts. I'd known them all my life. They were John Royd and his wife, and their young daughter, Julia—"

"Julia Royd?" asked Kelton.

The captain nodded.

"Yes, the same," he said. "I'd known her since she was a baby—a few years younger than myself. We'd played together as lad and lass. When I went away she was just a pretty little kid in short dresses, still playing with dolls. But when I came back she was a young woman, with her hair done up—and before that evening at John Royd's farm was over, I knew I was in love with Julia Royd. I knew something else—from her eyes. She loved me. That month I stayed in Abbott's Glade was the finest, happiest time of my life. I saw Julia every day and there were picnics, and hay-rides, and walks and talks in the moonlight, and with every day we fell more deeply in love with each other. Before three weeks had passed she had promised to marry me. I was beside myself with joy. We talked it over and her parents and mine, and they were well pleased. We talked of getting married at once, but the older ones were against it. Julia and I were young, they said, and could wait a year or so until I had gained the promotion which was coming to me after another trip. I expected to be gone about a year—on a trip round the Horn—and I consented to wait. My heart was heavy when I said good-bye to Julia, and yet I was happy. In a year I'd return and take her with me as my bride. She kissed me good-bye at the little Abbott's Glade station—and off I went to join my ship."

The captain paused, drew at his pipe, and went on. "I had a grand voyage—Sao Paulo, San Francisco, Singapore—and finally back to Dundee. I'd written to Julia from every port and sent her little presents, and had a few letters from her, warm, loving letters they were—though she, like most Yorkshire folk, was no great hand at writing. I skipped off my ship at Dundee, a furlough in my pocket, and gold, too, a neat new uniform on my back, and my heart beating high. It seemed to take the train forever and a day to get to Abbott's Glade where I knew Julia would be waiting for me. I jumped out of the train before it had stopped. I was so eager to run to her house and take her in my arms. I hadn't let her know I was coming, you see. I wanted to surprise her. She had last heard from me when the ship was coaling at Bombay—and at that time I thought I wouldn't get home for five or six months.

"Well, I did run to her house—and she was there—and as soon as I saw her I knew something was wrong. She kissed me, and tried to pretend she was glad to see me—but I knew her laughter was forced. I tried to get her to tell me if anything was amiss, and for a while she insisted there wasn't, and then, suddenly, she broke down and began to cry and she told me—"

The captain bit his words off short. His face was working with emotion.

"It was the old story—a story you'll hear I suppose, as long as there are men and women in the world. In my absence Julia had met another man. I'll call him a man—though he wasn't. Mr. Kelton, if there ever was a beast in man's form it was Jacob Murdo. He was a big, rather handsome fellow, older than me by a few years. He came from York, and he traveled about the country, selling ploughs, harrows and other farming implements to the farmers.

A shrewd man, everyone said, and bound to rise in the
world. Already he was pushing toward a partnership in
his firm. He seemed to be one of those men who is bound
to get ahead—for he had no end of self-confidence, and
a masterful way with him. Well, you can guess the rest.
He saw Julia—and he wanted her. He knew how to get
what he wanted—whether it was money or women. Julia
slapped his face—once—but he came back again, and he
kept coming back. He told her he was in love with her,
that he wanted to marry her, and painted a picture of an
easy life with him in York, the life of the wife of a rich
man. Still she resisted him—on my account—though he
laughed at her and told her she was a fool to throw her life
away by marrying a poor sailor. He didn't love her—he was
the sort of man who can love nobody but himself—but he
had made up his mind to have her, no matter what methods he had to use. When everything he tried had failed, he
told her a lie about me. He said, he had seen, in a Lloyd's
report that I had been lost at sea. Poor Julia—she believed
him. I couldn't find it in my heart to blame her. She was
just a lass, who'd never seen anything of the world, and
he was clever, damnably clever. Well, it ended with him
persuading her to elope to Edinburgh with him, where he
promised to marry her. Of course, once he got her there,
he did not keep his promise. He put her off. Finally, he
tired of her and sent her back home with a story that
she'd gone off to Edinburgh to work in one of the mills.
Her parents believed her, for she had always been a true,
honest girl—but—that terrible day—sitting on the bench
where she had pledged herself to marry me—she told me
that she could not keep her secret from them much longer. She was going to have a baby—his baby—that beast,
Murdo's."

The captain stopped. He could not continue for a moment.

"What did you do?" Matthew Kelton asked.

"I went crazy—for a while. I wanted to kill him. 1 wanted to feel my bare hands on his throat, crushing the life out of him. Julia begged me to be calm. The thing was done, she said, and could not be mended now. For me to kill Murdo would only mean putting my own neck in a noose, and bringing disgrace on her, her parents and mine. Well, I listened to her—and I've always regretted that I did. We talked it over. I said I'd marry her myself. She said she could not do that—that I'd only hate her for what she had done, her and the child. I told you, Mr. Kelton, that we are a simple people in Yorkshire. According to our code, the man who wrongs a girl must marry her. It's barbarous, I know, but it was what Julia and I had been taught to believe. I said I'd go to York and put the case before Jacob Murdo—and ask him to do the fair thing. I didn't know him then, you see. I believed what I wanted to believe, and that was that he had been honestly in love with Julia, and that circumstances had forced him to put off marrying her. I went to York to see him. It did not take me long to find out what he really was like. He sneered at me. 'If I married all the country lasses who fall in love with me,' he said, 'I'd have to set up a harem. Run along now.' Why I didn't kill him then and there, I don't know. I'd faithfully promised Julia to keep my hands in my pockets all through my interview with him—and I kept my word. I went out of his office, and when I came back I had a revolver in my pocket. I showed it to him, and his face went green, and I knew that for all his size, he was a coward. 'You are going to marry Julia Royd,' I said, 'and this very day, and give a name to her child, or I'm going to shoot you.' He was smart enough to see that I meant business. His manner changed. He really cared for Julia, he said, and had intended all along to marry her, but a rush of work had come along, and as he was in line for a partnership he had delayed and so forth. I half believed him. I wanted to believe him for Julia's sake. I didn't trust him however, and I marched him back to Abbott's Glade, my finger on the trigger all the way, and saw them properly married in the little stone church there, with my eyes blinded with tears and my heart sick and empty. Then I went away."

"Just before I went," continued Captain Galvin, "I had a private talk with Jacob Murdo. I told him, with all the force I could, that he had married the finest girl in Yorkshire, and that she would make him a wife any man could be proud of. I said to him, 'Jacob Murdo, you are going to be kind to her and take good care of her. If you are not, if you mistreat her in any way, then I swear by my hope of salvation, you will answer to me for it. I'll kill you,' I said. He was cowed by then, and he knew I meant every word I said. He promised to make Julia a good husband. I went off to Dundee and stayed drunk, rolling drunk, for two weeks, the first time I was ever drunk in my life. Then I joined my ship, and sailed off for Liberia and the Gold Coast to collect rubber and ivory."

The captain filled his pipe again.

"This is all ancient history, I know, Mr. Kelton, but it has to be told if you are to understand the case," he said. "That trip gave me no pleasure, but I did my work well. I was trying to forget, you see; but I knew I couldn't forget. I knew I loved Julia Royd and would always love her. I worked hard because work kept my mind active and sort of numbed the pain that was there. From the Gold Coast we went on to Cape Town, and then were in service between Cape Town and New Zealand. Time went by—but I didn't care. I had no wish to go back to Yorkshire. When I did go back—some three and a half years later—it was because of the death of my mother. I made guarded inquiries about Julia Royd. She had gone to York to live with her husband,

I learned, and there a child had been born to her, a son. I went to York, hoping for just a sight of her, nothing more. I felt I could never have a part in her life now. I could not find her. I began a search. At last from the neighbors, I learned what had happened. Murdo had not kept his promise to me. As soon as I was away at sea, even before the child was born, he began to treat Julia badly. After the child was born, he was worse. The neighbors said he beat her—"

The captain's big hands were knotted into hard fists.

"I could not keep my promise to him," he said, "because he had left York. When the boy was two years old, he deserted Julia, leaving her sick and without a penny. He went away—nobody knew where—and he took the baby with him. He had struck Julia, knocking her senseless when she fought to keep the baby, saying 'It's my child. He'll be a rich man's son.' It came out soon enough why Jacob Murdo had fled from York. He had been stealing from his firm, and when he left he took some two thousand pounds of the firm's money with him. A search was made, of course, and you know the English police are efficient, but Murdo slipped through their fingers. They got no trace of him at all. Poor Julia—her parents had died, and she was deserted, crushed, and half crazed with grief at the loss of the little boy. God, if I'd only got back a month sooner. But I didn't, and just a month before I arrived in York, Julia went to search for her child. No one could tell me where she had gone."

The captain wiped the sweat from his brow.

"The story skips a good many years now," he said. "I had to go off to sea again—sailing to every corner of the world—for the sea was my only means of making a living. Everywhere I went I made inquiries about Julia Royd, and about Murdo and the child. When I had leave, I went to inland cities, hunting. The world is a big place, Mr. Kelton.

I did not find her. I did not even find a trail I could follow. So the years went by, and Julia was never entirely out of my mind or my heart. I put advertisements in the papers—wherever I went—but they were never answered. Many times my reason told me to give up hope—but I wouldn't. That's the way Yorkshire men are, Mr. Kelton. Love, with them, is stronger than death. So time passed, as I said, and I became a captain with a ship of my own and I was proud, but never a day went by that I did not think, 'Where is Julia? If I only had her—sailing with me—' Then we started—it seems like a year ago though it is only a few hours—on this ill-fated trip.

"I was standing on the bridge, watching the preparations to cast off, and watching, sort of absently, the passengers come up the gang-plank. Then I saw a man coming aboard—and my heart stopped beating. He was older, stouter, grayer—but his face had burned itself into my memory, and I knew that one of my passengers was—Jacob Murdo. I turned away. He had not seen me. I went to my cabin—hardly knowing what I was doing—and read the passenger list. From the purser I learned that Murdo was booked under the name of Samuel P. Cleghorn. I could see the reason for that. As soon as he left York, he took a new name. He wanted, naturally, to throw the police off the track. I hadn't a doubt in the world that under his new name he had settled in America and had prospered. My brain was all jumbled. What was I to do? He might know where Julia was. He probably knew what had become of the child. But if he saw me, he'd be sure to recognize me, and he'd be on his guard; or he would flee off the ship and be lost again. I stayed in my cabin till the ship had cleared the harbor, debating what I'd do. Then I made up my mind. I'd go down and face Murdo. I'd get the truth out of him, about Julia, if I could. If I couldn't, I'd punish him for what he had done to her. It was reckless, insane—

but I did not think of that. It would cost me my ship, perhaps my liberty—but I remembered Julia's trusting, gentle
face—and with my heart banging inside me, I went down
to the cabin of Jacob Murdo—or Samuel P. Cleghorn."

"What time was this?" asked Kelton.

"About half an hour after we passed the Statue of Liberty," replied Captain Galvin. "Well, I pushed open his
cabin door without knocking and there he was. He knew
me at once. I saw that he did. His cruel eyes widened and
the color left his face.

"He tried to bluff. 'What can I do for you, Captain,'
he said. 'You can tell me what has become of Julia, Jacob
Murdo,' I said. 'You're mistaken,' he said. 'My name is
Cleghorn.' 'You're lying,' I said. 'Do you think I could
forget you in twenty years or twenty centuries? Tell me
what you know of her, while you have the breath to speak.'
He was yellow. 'I know nothing of her, David Galvin,'
he said. 'I have had no word from her since I left York. I
have looked for her everywhere. I did her a great wrong,
and I wanted to make amends.' I knew he was lying. I
could see behind those rattish eyes that he was playing for
time, trying to stall me off till he could make a break for
safety. 'You remember what I told you in the church-yard
at Abbott's Glade,' I said, and I knew from his face that
he remembered. Then, without warning, he caught up a
heavy blackthorn stick he had carried aboard, and hurled
himself at me. I was in the doorway, barring his path. I
broke the force of the stick's blow with my forearms, and
we clinched. He was strong, but I was stronger, and my
hate was hot within me. I got the stick away from him and
hit him, hit him again and again, till he lay in a bloody
heap at my feet. Then I was like a man waking from a
nightmare. I saw what I had done. I lifted him and put
him in his berth and drew the curtains. I threw the stick
out of the porthole and closed the porthole. I would have

thrown his body out, too, but it would not go through. I
had no plan. I did whatever came into my confused mind.
Then I heard sounds in the corridor, and thought it might
be the steward who would catch me; so I dashed out of the
cabin and up to the deck."

"What then?"

"I was running along the corridor when I saw a woman
standing outside Cabin B, where Murdo lay. My first
thought was that she must have heard the sounds of the
fight. My next thought was that I knew her. Years had
changed her, but a man never forgets the face of the girl he
first loved. At the same instant I saw Julia Royd, she saw
me. She gave a cry and started toward me. All my instincts
told me that I must get away from the vicinity of Cabin
B, so I started to run again, knowing she would follow.
Well, perhaps you'll remember I collided with you on the
stairs?"

"Yes, I remember," said Matthew Kelton. "So did Miss
Royd."

"She had half-fainted when she saw me," said the captain, "and as soon as she recovered she ran after me. She
came to my cabin. The meeting I had yearned for all those
years took place—but it was a bitter meeting for both of
us. I told her—I knew I'd have to tell her sooner or later—
of my meeting with Murdo, or Cleghorn, and what I had
done. She said she would stand by me. I cannot say the
deed weighed very heavily on my conscience. Murdo had
struck me first, and I had had to defend myself. I felt, too,
that the world was a better place with him out of it. Certainly, if any man deserved his fate it was Jacob Murdo. I
knew of course that the law does not countenance murder
or manslaughter. It would mean prison and ruin for me if
I was caught—just when I had found Julia. So we decided
to trust to luck that I would not be caught. Probably there
were plenty of men who hated a man like Murdo enough

to want to kill him. We decided, Julia and I, that I would come forward and tell the truth only if it was necessary to do so to save an innocent man. That's what I'm doing now, Mr. Kelton. I cannot stand by and see Russell Sangerson accused of the crime—"

"Captain," said Matthew Kelton, "I'm greatly moved by what you have told me. But there is more—I know there is—"

"What more can there be?"

"It's obvious. What is your real motive for wanting to save Sangerson?"

"I think you know," Captain Galvin said, quietly. "At first I had no idea who Sangerson was. I did not know that he was connected with Murdo in any way. Then as you probably suspected I got hold of the cablegrams to you—and found out from them who Sangerson really is. He's not Murdo's nephew. He's his son—his son and Julia Royd's. I was sure of it when I saw Sangerson's eyes—they are his mother's eyes—as I remember them back in Abbott's Glade."

"But why should Murdo, or Cleghorn, pass his son off as his nephew?"

"To make it more difficult for the police to detect him, I suppose," said the captain. "Once he had started the fiction, he had to keep it up. He was always wily, Jacob Murdo was. Why he took the boy at all, and kept him, is harder to explain but I think I know why."

"Why?"

"Pride. Yorkshire men are full of it. They want sons to inherit their fortunes. They may treat their sons badly—as I've no doubt Murdo did his—but they want any money they accumulate to pass on to their own flesh and blood. I know Yorkshire men, and I'm sure I'm right."

"Does Julia Royd know that Sangerson is her son?"

Captain Galvin shook his head.

"It would be right to tell her, I suppose," he said. "But I haven't been able to make up my mind. You cannot think very clearly when you've done a murder and expect every minute to feel the hand of the law on your shoulder."

"Captain," said Matthew Kelton, "for the time being, don't tell her. She must be told—but not yet. Now I want to ask you something."

"Yes, Mr. Kelton."

"What time was it when you were in Cabin B?"

"About one o'clock, I'd say. Not much later, anyhow."

"Then how do you explain the fact that at five Larsen, the steward, distinctly heard Cleghorn's or Murdo's, voice in his cabin?"

The captain shook his head.

"I can't explain that at all," he said. "The only thing I can think of is the man with the eyes. Murdo's killing is accounted for, God help me—but the eyes are not. He—call him devil or what you please—may have been in the cabin for reasons of his own; but it wasn't Murdo's voice that answered the steward. He was dead when I left the cabin."

"I see," said Kelton, half to himself. "Then our one mystery splits into two separate ones."

Captain Galvin sat in his chair, his head slumped forward on his great chest.

"You've heard my story, Mr. Kelton," he said. "I suppose the thing to do is for me to navigate my ship into Hamilton harbor and then turn myself over to the police. I won't try to get away. I'll face the music. The Murdo case is finished. But we still have to find those eyes—"

A knock sounded on the door.

"Mr. Kelton in there?" asked the voice of Haley, the radio operator.

"Yes."

"Couple of messages for you."

"Thank you, Haley," said Matthew Kelton, opening the door and taking the messages.

One was in code. Without stopping to figure it out, he thrust it into his pocket. The other was brief. It read, simply.

"Yes. Tyne."

Kelton smothered an oath.

"The old dodo," he exclaimed. "Why couldn't he have been more specific?"

"What?" asked the captain.

"Never mind. Talking to myself," said Kelton. "Captain, I'm going to find those eyes for you—this very night. It's not going to be easy—and it's going to be dangerous. What firearms have you aboard?"

"Not many. I have an automatic pistol, and I think McQuarrie has an old army revolver and there's a shot-gun in the purser's office, left there by some passenger—Great Heavens, what's that?"

The captain and Kelton had both leaped up from their seats. What they heard was a human voice—screaming frightfully.

"Quick," snapped Kelton. "We may be in time. Oh, why was I such a dumb fool? I was afraid this would happen. Got your pistol, Captain?"

"Right here—ready," cried the captain, and he rushed out of the cabin, Kelton at his heels.

14
The Fate of Gabe Festy Able Seaman

The cries had stopped. They had, apparently, come from some point on the upper deck, near the stern. It was a dark night, filled with the velvet blackness which comes to the semi-tropics. Captain Galvin's electric torch made a white path along the deck. Toward the stern, beneath a lifeboat, he and Kelton stopped, and from both of them came a cry of horror. In the path of the light lay the body of a man.

"Who is it?" Kelton asked, and he could hardly enunciate.

"Can't tell. Kelton, this is ghastly. He's been horribly mangled—"

The light played on the shapeless mass on the deck.

"It's the sailor, Fest," said Kelton in a whisper.

"Yes. It's Fest. Quite dead."

The captain knelt beside the body.

"Who could have done this? A poor inoffensive negro sailor! Look, Kelton, how terribly he has been beaten. His chest and head are crushed. Why, even his legs are broken."

"Oh, how stupid I've been," groaned Kelton. "I'll never be proud of my intelligence again. I might have prevented this. Captain—"

"What?"

"There isn't a second to lose. Go below. Get that shotgun. Bring it here. I'll stand guard by the body. Give me

your pistol. I won't take time to explain—but hurry back
with that shot-gun. Give your officers orders to have every
man and women on board either lock themselves in some
safe place, or arm themselves and be ready. Unless I'm
wrong there is a killer on board, running amok, and apt
to appear anywhere, any second. I haven't time to tell you
what I suspect—Hurry. It's a matter of life and death—"

The captain, unquestioningly, sped away. Kelton swung
himself up to the lifeboat, very cautiously. The tarpaulin
had been torn aside. Fest had clearly been dragged from
his improvised bed to be beaten to death on the deck below. On the edge of the lifeboat, Kelton perched, his finger on the trigger of the automatic, and in his other hand
the captain's electric torch, extinguished, but ready to be
switched on by the pressure of a thumb. He heard the captain's steps as he hastened back toward the lifeboat.

"Quick," said Kelton, in a low tense voice. "Up here,
beside me. Hand me that shot-gun. You take the pistol.
Now, for the love of Heaven, don't make a sound."

"Are you going to leave the body lying there?" whispered
the captain. He climbed up to the lifeboat and crouched
there beside Kelton.

"Sssssssssh. Not a sound. Leave it to me. The body
must be left there. You'll see why—very soon—unless I'm
wrong."

In the black silence they waited. The minutes crawled
by. Once the captain, holding his lips close to Kelton's ear,
whispered, "What's the idea?"

Kelton's reply was "Sssssh, for God's sake."

Then, in the blackness, the waiting men heard a sound.
It was a curious sound, a rustling, and scraping, and a faint
creaking of the iron stair leading to the deck. Something
was coming up those stairs. Slowly, surely, nearer, nearer.

Captain Galvin's fingers convulsively clutched Kelton's
arm.

"Look," he whispered.

In the darkness at the head of the stairs, two eyes gleamed. They were six feet or more above the deck. Then, slowly, the eyes moved across the deck toward the lifeboat.

In the tense hush of the night Kelton could hear the captain's heart thumping. Nearer drew the eyes.

They were within a yard of where the body of the sailor lay when Kelton whispered.

"Quick. Turn on the light."

The white beam of the flashlight cut through the blackness. Then Matthew Kelton fired the shot-gun, both barrels. The flashlight beam quivered insanely in Captain Galvin's trembling hand.

"Great God," he said, "a snake!"

"Don't move," cried Kelton. "He may not be dead."

In the beam of light a giant snake writhed in a death agony; then all motion stopped, and the long body lay still.

"Look," said the captain. "He's dead. You blew his head off."

He and Kelton scrambled down.

The sound of the shots had brought First Officer McQuarrie and several sailors to the scene, lanterns in their hands.

"Stand back," directed the captain.

"He'll do no more harm," said Matthew Kelton. "He's done enough, Heaven knows. Will someone notify the doctor to take charge of poor Fest's body. His murderer lies beside him."

"Throw the snake into the sea," ordered the captain. "Kelton, I've got to get back to my cabin. I'm shot to pieces. I've got to have a drink."

Back in the captain's cabin, Matthew Kelton was despondent. He heaped reproaches on himself.

"I guessed what it was—this afternoon," he said. "If I'd only acted on my guess, I might have saved that poor fellow's life. Too late now. Why didn't I see at once that it was the work of an anaconda. Those scales should have told me—even if reasoning didn't.'"

"An anaconda? So that's what it was?"

His drink of rum had steadied the captain's nerves a trifle.

"Yes. Part of Professor Tyne's collection. After his shipwreck he had no time to check up on just what animals and snakes he had, and this one got away and wasn't missed on the voyage. Yes, an anaconda, thirty feet long, and strong as any living thing. They live in trees and hunt for their prey at night. They're noted for their intelligence and craftiness. This one, apparently, soon adapted himself to life on shipboard. By day, he hid, probably along the steam pipes in the engine room. No wonder your men, looking for a man or a devil, overlooked him. By night he stole out through the ship. He made no sound. He picked dark places and moved stealthily, for he was a trained hunter. If he heard someone near he had only to remain motionless to be mistaken for a rope or a hose; or he could slip away with incredible speed at the approach of danger. When he raised his head erect, his eyes were some six feet from the ground, and it was that which gave Miss Cobb, and Fest the idea that it was a tall man, and fooled me, too. It was certainly the anaconda which hung over the rail and looked through Miss Yate's porthole. Lucky thing for her it was closed. She was right in describing his eyes as hypnotic. That's a little aid Nature has given him to get his prey. A snake like that can hypnotize an animal—a deer, or a wild pig, or even a jaguar—so that it cannot move, and the snake can crush it in his coils and devour it. Why the snake was content with knocking Miss Cobb down with one blow of his powerful head, and then leaving her, I don't know. Frightened, probably. She might easily have shared Caesar's fate. Fest saw him in the bunk-room last night—and sought to escape by jumping into the sea. Poor fellow, he might better have been drowned. Fate, it would seem, had marked him as prey for the monster."

"I didn't know they attacked men," said the captain.

"They don't, ordinarily. But remember this creature was ravenously hungry. In this condition, a member of the boa family, will attack any living thing. He was prowling about on deck—he could see in the dark, of course—when he heard Fest snoring in his lifeboat. And Fest had gone there for safety! Ironic, isn't it? Once the anaconda had spotted his prey, Fest hadn't a chance. The strongest man that ever lived would be like a child's wooden soldier in the grip of such a brute. A twist and a squeeze and every bone in a man's body would be broken."

"How did you know the snake would come back?" asked the captain.

"I wasn't sure. It was a guess. I figured that he had been frightened off by hearing us coming and seeing our light. Therefore, he was still hungry. The chances were that when he thought the coast was clear, he'd return to his kill, to crush it into a size he could devour. That's what he did—and we'll hear no more about the eyes."

"When you got that radiogram, you were sure it was a snake, weren't you?"

"Not positive. I wired Professor Tyne to-day asking him if he had missed any snake or large animal. The exasperating old idiot wired back 'yes.' Nobody can be more inexact than a scientific man when he is not interested."

Captain Galvin was leaning forward on his desk, his head bowed over on his folded arms.

"I'm terribly, terribly tired," he said. "I haven't closed my eyes since we left New York. I think I can sleep now. I have squared my account with Jacob Murdo, and I have told you my story, and I'm now ready to square my account with the law."

"Captain," said Matthew Kelton, "you go ahead and get ready for bed. I'll stay a minute or two more, if you don't mind. I want to talk to you."

"There isn't much to talk about now—" said the captain, as he began to undress. "Your duty is plain, Mr. Kelton. I suppose that since the crime was committed in American waters, I'll be turned over to the detective who came down on the *Tarragonno*. She'll be in a few hours ahead of us, I've heard by radio."

He had taken off his uniform coat and his shirt, revealing thick, powerful arms and heavy, hairy forearms. Kelton was watching him.

"Captain," he said, "you'll remember we have one minor mystery to clear up."

"What's that?" asked the captain, reaching for his pajamas.

"The voice in Cabin B—about five o'clock," said Kelton. "You thought it had something to do with the eyes. But the eyes belong to a snake, and snakes cannot talk."

"It doesn't matter much," said the captain, yawning. "Just now sleep is the only thing that matters to me. Sleep—and lots of it. To-morrow I'm in for one of the worst days of my life."

"Don't be so sure of that, Captain."

"Why, what do you mean?"

"I'll let you know to-morrow—maybe," said Matthew Kelton. "Good night."

Kelton went back to his own cabin. He felt let down and weary. He was thinking about the captain's story, and his confession. What stand could he take, ethically, in the matter? Doubtless Cleghorn, or Jacob Murdo, had been an evil character, and no ornament to the world, but murder is murder—and Kelton knew that the New York detective who stepped aboard the *Pendragon* in Hamilton would make an arrest, if for no better reason than to earn the five thousand dollar reward. The reasoning of the detective would be sure to lead him to arrest Russell Sangerson. He'd know about Sangerson's relationship to Cleghorn, of course, and perhaps about their quarrel. He'd reason that Sangerson had a strong motive—the inheritance of a large fortune on the death of Cleghorn. Yes, assuredly, Sangerson would be arrested—and then Captain Galvin would come forward to save the son of the woman he loved.

The captain might get off with a light sentence for manslaughter but his career would be utterly ruined, and Kelton felt that in the circumstances this was a harsher fate than the captain deserved.

"There are just two things which make me think there may be hope for the captain," Kelton said to himself. "One is a very trivial matter—a tuft of hair. Since my gorilla turned out to be an anaconda, that tuft of hair I found in Cabin B is not accounted for. It couldn't have been there when Cleghorn came aboard. I've watched Larsen, and he does a very thorough job of cleaning. A blotch like that on the washstand could not be overlooked. Therefore it got there after Cleghorn moved into his cabin. It's up to me to find out where it came from and what it signifies.

"And there's another odd thing," mused Kelton.

"The captain stated that Cleghorn, or Murdo, struck him on his forearms—and there were no bruises, black and blue spots or other marks on them, as there certainly would be if he really was hit with a blackthorn stick. By jingo, if the captain lying, too? Is his confession a fake like the rest of them? There's one person who may be able to throw some light on that—and that is Miss Julia Royd."

He had begun to get ready for bed. Now he threw on his clothes again. He knew himself well enough to know that he could never get to sleep while an important question—for which he knew how to find the answer—was tormenting his mind.

On tiptoes he went round to Cabin A, and very gently knocked on the door.

"Who is it?"

He recognized Julia Royd's whispered voice.

"It's Matthew Kelton," he answered. "I must speak to you. Will you come to my cabin?"

It was no time for etiquette or the proprieties. Miss Yate, as he had surmised, had taken her sleeping potion and gone to sleep.

"What do you want of me?" asked Julia Royd.

"I want to ask you a few questions."

"What about?"

"About Captain Galvin."

"I'll come," answered Julia Royd, at once. Presently, wrapped in her blue cloak, she was sitting in Cabin C, looking at Matthew Kelton with anxious eyes.

"I do not want you to be alarmed, Miss Royd," Matthew Kelton began. "I am trying to act as a friend toward you and Captain Galvin."

"What has he said?"

"You know what he has said," returned Kelton. "I have just now returned from his cabin. I spent most of the evening there. The captain and I had a long talk. You can guess, I think, what it was about. Miss Royd, I want to ask you one question. Do you believe that Captain Galvin killed Jacob Murdo?"

He looked at her steadily.

Her eyes did not waver.

"Did he say he did?" she asked.

"He did."

"Did he tell you the whole story?"

"He did."

"About Abbott's Glade—and all the rest?"

"Yes. Miss Royd, I think he kept back nothing."

"I think he did."

"What?"

"The name of the person who really killed Jacob Murdo."

"And you know it?"

"Yes."

15

WHAT JULIA ROYD KNEW

"It wasn't the captain, then?" asked Matthew Kelton.

"It was not."

"Who was it?"

She did not drop her eyes. She looked back at him, her head held high.

"It was I," she said. "David Galvin is in no way guilty— he is simply shouldering the blame which should rest on me alone."

"You did it?"

"If you know my story, can you blame me?" she returned.

"It is not I who have to blame you, or absolve you," said Matthew Kelton.

"You know why I did it—or part of the reason. You cannot know—no one but I can know—what I suffered at the hands of Jacob Murdo. Perhaps David has told you about—about the early days."

"Yes, he has."

"Even David does not know—everything," she said. "Oh, he knows I was beaten. I've the scars, still. But I alone know the scars Jacob Murdo left on my soul. Taking my baby—which I loved—even though it was his—"

She pressed her lips together.

"Yes, and a hundred other indignities, humiliations, cruelties. He liked to see me cry. He said so, often. Well—as you say—it is not for you to judge whether or not I was justified. You want to know what I did."

Kelton inclined his head.

"When I left York," Julia Royd said, "I was a crushed woman. My father had left me a little money—a few hundred pounds; so I was able to start out in search of my baby. I came to New York, steerage. Jacob Murdo had often threatened to leave me. 'I'll go to the States,' he used to say, 'where the big money is.' Money—it's all he ever cared about. I could not find him in New York. I searched—everywhere, until my money was gone,—and then I got a job as a nurse maid. I pretended it was my own baby I was taking care of. The family I worked for was very kind to me. They were of Yorkshire stock, originally, themselves, and they made me almost one of the family. When they moved out near Calgary, in Canada, to a ranch they took me along to take care of the two little girls. I went, because I was weary of searching, searching, searching. Murdo might have gone to Australia—or South America—and I had no money to keep up the search. I stayed in Calgary many years. I was not happy, but the people were kind, and it was the only home I had. Then they moved back to New York to put the girls—they're young ladies now—in college—and I had no work to do. At their house I met Miss Yate, who is a distant connection of theirs, and she offered me a position as nurse and traveling companion. Two weeks ago I went with her, and, suddenly, she decided to take a trip to Bermuda. Of course I accompanied her. I saw that she was settled comfortably in her cabin, and I went out to look after some of her luggage which hadn't been sent to the cabin. I had just stepped out of the corridor—when I ran into—Jacob Murdo. He recognized me at once—and I knew him. I could see it was a shock. He looked pretty sick at seeing me. 'Come into my cabin,' he said. 'Let's talk things over.' I went. I wanted news of my child. He adopted his old bullying manner once we were safely behind a door. He said, 'I suppose you'll try to blackmail me. Well, I'll make you an allowance—a hundred dollars a month—to keep your mouth shut.' I had been frightened of him in the old days—but I wasn't then. I demanded that he tell me what had become of the baby. 'Oh, he died years ago,' he said. Then he threw the old accusation at me—the one he used to make in the old days in York when he wanted to make me cry—'I was never sure he was mine, anyhow,' he said. 'He might have been that sailor fellow's, or any of the lads about Abbott's Glade.' It was a shameful lie, and I was wild with rage, and began to call him names. He said, 'Stop that. You can't threaten me. I have money and position—and you're nothing. Try blackmailing me, and I'll crush you. Now get out.' He took me by the arm to put me out of the cabin. Well, I'm strong. I've done hard work all my life. I hit him—with all my might—between the eyes."

"What with?"

"Some sort of club."

"How did you happen to be carrying a club?"

"I wasn't. I—I—picked it up in the cabin. He snarled and rushed at me and I struck him again. I think I must have been insane. I may have struck him a dozen times—I don't know. Then I ran out of the cabin."

"What time was this?"

"Very soon after the ship left the pier—about twenty minutes, I think."

"I see. After you left the cabin, what did you do?"

"I went back to Cabin A."

"And then?"

"Miss Yate asked me to go out to see if I could find a small bag of hers that was missing—the one I had started out to find before. As I stepped out of the cabin, a man passed down the corridor—he stopped and looked at me—and it was David Galvin. I thought he recognized me, but I wasn't sure—for he ran away. I was overcome for a minute or two, and then I hurried after him—"

"Colliding with me on the way," put in Kelton.

"Was it you? I was too upset to see clearly. You see, Mr. Kelton, I've always loved David Galvin. I'd hoped that sometime, somehow, we'd meet again. I didn't try to find him. I had done him a great wrong—and I was ashamed of it. I didn't think he could love me—after what happened. Well, even as I hurried along, I seemed to know what had occurred. David had recognized Murdo when he came aboard. David had gone down to the cabin to give him a thrashing, possibly even to kill him. But when David got to Cabin B, Murdo had already been killed. David must have known that I did it. What he did in the cabin, I don't know. We talked it over—the death, I mean—and agreed that if the fact of who the man was who called himself Cleghorn came out, David or I might be suspected, so we'd better say nothing and hope that it would be an unsolved mystery."

"And you agreed to speak out only if some innocent person was accused; is that right?"

"Yes; that's right," answered Julia Royd. "We were terribly worried, of course. We wanted to talk together—to comfort each other, but it was difficult. Perhaps you don't know that last night, while you were visiting the captain, I was hidden in his closet."

"Were you indeed?" said Matthew Kelton.

"I was—and I nearly smothered, too. Well, it would have saved a lot of trouble if I had. I don't care about myself—it's David I'm thinking of. He's loved me—all these years—and searched for me. Men like David Galvin are rare in this world, Mr. Kelton."

"All too rare," said Matthew Kelton. "Tell me, Miss Royd, what did you do with the club you say you used?"

"Why, I—I—threw it away."

"Where?"

"Into the sea."

"Through the porthole?"

She hesitated.

"No. I threw it over the rail."

"Then you must have had it when you collided with me?"

"Yes—I did."

"I didn't see it."

"It was hidden under my cloak."

"I see."

He studied her a moment.

"Miss Royd," he said, "you have my sympathy. I'm going to do everything in my power to help you. I don't, as a rule, condone murder, but in this case, I'm going to try to get justice for you. I'm going to ask you to let me take charge of your case. You will have to be arrested, and stand trial, of course, but I know a lawyer who will tell your story to a jury so that they will see Murdo as you saw him—and I think an American jury will be lenient with you."

"I'm grateful to you, Mr. Kelton," Miss Royd said, impassively. "I'm not worrying about the consequences of my act. I have broken the law—and I am ready to be punished. I don't think that there's anything more to say."

She rose.

"Just a moment before you go, please," said Kelton. "I've another question I'd like to ask you."

"Well?"

"It's about Miss Yate."

Her face hardened.

"What do you want to know about her?"

"I want to know where she was yesterday—say between the time she came aboard and six o'clock?'

"In her cabin," replied Julia Royd.

"Are you sure of that?"

"Yes."

"You can't be positive, Miss Royd."

"Why not?"

"You've just told me that you spent at least part of the afternoon talking with Captain Galvin in his cabin. Now, after all those years of separation, and with so much to talk about and decide about, I can't believe that you were away from Cabin A a short time. As a matter of fact, you were away from Cabin A most of the afternoon, weren't you?"

"Perhaps I was. But Miss Yate was in her cabin!"

"How do you know she was?"

"She said so."

"Ah, that's another matter. Now, were you in the cabin from quarter to five to half-past?"

"No. I wasn't. I was taking a bath."

"Then if Miss Yate was out of her cabin at that time you wouldn't know about it, would you?"

"No. But I don't see what all these questions are about. Miss Yate has nothing to do with this case. She's a very kind woman, and she's an invalid. Why are you questioning me about her?"

"Because I'm trying to find out something," replied Matthew Kelton. "I want you to tell me more about her— and her illness—"

"I do not feel I have the right to discuss her private affairs," said Julia Royd.

"Even if by so doing you may be able to save her from an embarrassing, perhaps dangerous, predicament?" asked Kelton.

"What do you mean?"

"Suppose Miss Yate were to be charged with a very grave offense?"

"You don't mean murder. How could she have anything to do with it—when I did it—myself."

"I don't mean murder—exactly," said Kelton. "There are other grave offenses against the law, you know. Come now, Miss Royd, I appreciate your loyalty to Miss Yate, but there are times when loyalty may throw sand in the eyes of justice. Since you won't tell me about her, I'm going to tell you—and, believe me, it will be for the best if you will tell me if I'm right."

She listened, carefully, while Matthew Kelton spoke. When he had finished, Julia Royd nodded.

"You're right," she said. "But I don't see that it has anything to do with the case."

"You may see to-morrow," said Matthew Kelton. "Now, good night, Miss Royd, and remember this. Justice is often clumsy, stupid, near-sighted, but I've been watching its wheels go round for a good many years, and it's really quite astonishing how few people who are really guilty get away, and how few who are really innocent are punished."

"When will they arrest me?" asked Julia Royd.

"Well, not to-night, anyhow," said Matthew Kelton. "Please try to get some sleep. Take one of those sleeping powders—if you have to. To-morrow will be plenty of time to think about getting arrested. Now, good night."

He held out his hand to her.

"You've been brave for a good many years," he said. "Try to be brave just a few hours longer."

Julia Royd took his hand.

"Talking to you has made me feel easier in my mind," she said. "Thank you, Mr. Kelton. Good night."

The door closed behind her.

Matthew Kelton looked, yearningly, at his bed.

"Not yet a while," he muttered. "There are a few points I want to run over. First, why did Julia Royd lie about that club she said she used? She said she had it with her when she bumped into me in the hall. My memory is better than hers. I remember distinctly that she put out both hands to keep from falling. She had no club then, surely. Question—was there a club? Oh, well, this ship is chock full of earnest liars—and none of them seems to know the job."

He pulled out of his pocket the radiogram he had received from Mr. B. Hong, and which he had not had time to read. He studied it, with creased brow.

The radiogram read:

"Are monkey silver vest canoe wall truck cattle-
man needle panther dish aspen poker spike
yes are oil tumbril essence pond goat.
"Hong."

Matthew Kelton and Mr. Hong had a private code, agreed on years before, so in a short time, with a stub of a pencil and a sheet of paper, Kelton decoded the message. He read it through three times. He sat motionless for half an hour.

Then he went to bed, observing, "To-morrow promises to be quite a day."

16
What Matthew Kelton Knew

The S.S. *Pendragon* stopped off St. George's, Bermuda, late that morning. It stopped only long enough for the mail boat to come alongside and take off a few sacks of mail. St. George's, the old capital of the island, which looks like a medieval hill town in Italy, with its picturesque old houses, white and gray in the morning sun, is at the tip end of the island. Bermuda is some twenty miles long, and near the other end lies the new capital, newer and sprucer than St. George's—Hamilton. By steamer Hamilton is about an hour's run from St. George's. The steamers, usually, stop briefly at St. George's and then skirt along the palm-fringed coral island to Hamilton, where, after pushing into the narrow neck of the harbor, they dock.

When the postal launch drew alongside of the S.S. *Pendragon* at St. George's that day, the passengers, watching on deck, saw that the launch contained two passengers in civilian clothes, in addition to the uniformed representatives of the postal service.

A small gang-plank was lowered, and the two men in civilian clothes came aboard the *Pendragon,* looking business-like and grave.

Matthew Kelton, standing on deck, recognized one of the men at once—Detective Sergeant August Rudolph of the homicide squad of the New York Police Force, who

looked more like an actor playing the role of a detective,
than like a real one. He was a real one, however, as Kelton
from experience knew. Kelton considered him a keen young
man, even if he did wear rather noticeable suits and highly
colored shirts and ties. The other man, Kelton surmised,
was Mr. Roe, one of the partners of the dead Murdo, alias
Cleghorn, who had come by fast steamer to assist in the
investigation, and to take charge of the arrangements for
Cleghorn's funeral.

Detective-Sergeant Rudolph saw Matthew Kelton at
once, and promptly gave him a well-concealed wink. That
wink asked, "Do you want to let it be known that I know
you, or are you working under cover?"

Matthew Kelton's answer was to go to Detective-Sergeant
Rudolph, and shake him warmly by the hand.

"Glad to see you, Rudolph," he said.

"And I certainly am glad to see you," said the detective.
"If you've been aboard, there isn't going to be a thing for
me to do. Well, hand over the man. I can park him in the
local jail a few days while I look over the island."

"I'm not quite ready to do that," said Kelton with a
laugh. "I didn't expect you to come aboard till we got into
Hamilton."

"Thought I'd save time by hopping on at St. George's,"
said Rudolph. "By the way, Mr. Kelton, I want you to meet
Mr. Roe."

Matthew Kelton shook hands with Cleghorn's partner,
a ruddy faced, youngish man.

"It's a sad errand you're on," remarked Kelton.

"Yes," Mr. Roe agreed, "we'll miss Mr. Cleghorn. There
were very few more capable executives in New York than
he. It was a shock to all of us—this business. Did I understand you to say that you've made an arrest?"

"Not yet."

"You've got the man spotted?"

"I think so."

"That's good. None of us in New York could figure it out at all."

"Had Cleghorn no enemies?"

"No, I think not. Business rivals, of course. But nowadays business men cut prices, not throats."

"I understand that your firm has offered a reward for the arrest of the murderer."

"Yes. Five thousand dollars. Mr. Becker, the other partner and I, are offering it, jointly."

"I'm afraid I won't get a chance to cut in on it, if Kelton's been on the job," observed Detective-Sergeant Rudolph, gloomily.

"Well, you'll have had the trip, anyway," said Kelton.

"But will I take a prisoner back with me? That's what's on my mind just now," said the detective. He looked expectantly at Kelton.

"It's quite possible," said Kelton, with a smile. He noticed the detective give a slight start. Down the deck, the figure of Mr. Westervelt had passed. It seemed to Kelton that Mr. Westervelt had seen the detective, and had promptly turned his back, and gone indoors again. Kelton said nothing.

"What's the next move, Kelton?" Detective-Sergeant Rudolph inquired. "We're under way again and we'll be in Hamilton before long. Let's have the fellow. I don't want to have to play hide-and-seek with him all over the island."

"Take it easy, Rudolph," said Matthew Kelton. "I'm calling a little conference in the dining saloon. I've already sent out invitations to those I wish to attend. Perhaps you and Mr. Roe would like to be on hand. It may prove interesting."

"Another one of your little shows, eh?" said Detective-Sergeant Rudolph, with a chuckle. "I've attended 'em before, and they're always good. Plenty of suspense and a whacking good climax—not like a lot of the tripe I've been paying to see on Broadway."

"When did a New York cop ever pay to see a show?" Kelton asked, mildly.

"Well, I've gone to 'em, anyway," amended Rudolph. "Now, let's see what you have to offer."

"Come along then. This way, Mr. Roe," said Kelton.

They went to the dining saloon. Around the table the other passengers were grouped, waiting in strained silence. All of them were present—Mr. and Mrs. Johnstone, the three schoolteachers, Mr. Westervelt, Mr. Mond, the captain, the purser, the doctor, Miss Imlay, Russell Sangerson, Julia Royd, and Mr. Varga, who sat glowering at one end of the table. They were all there—except Miss Esther Yate. The New York detective and Mr. Roe found seats near the table, and watched the spectacle with interested eyes.

"Ladies and gentlemen," began Matthew Kelton, in a somewhat professorial manner, "I must ask you to excuse me for the rather theatrical aspect of this meeting. I can only say that I have thought it the best way to handle the situation. I know that you will bear with me—while I tell you my idea about the death of Mr. Cleghorn."

He looked about blandly. He had no need to ask them for their attention.

"I am going to tell you the whole story—as I see it," he said, "omitting nothing I consider important. When I finish, I hope you will agree with me."

"You'd think he was going to deliver a lecture on the life of Longfellow," murmured Mr. Mond in Miss Cobb's ear. He received a withering look in reply.

"The killing of Mr. Cleghorn," went on Matthew Kelton, "presented the most intricate problem I have ever tried to solve. It was full of complicating factors. The first of these was the appearance of a pair of gleaming eyes, which

I, not very brightly, I'll admit, connected with a man, and so, with the crime. You all know about the eyes now, and the tragedy of the death of the poor sailor, and the killing of the anaconda. Until I was able to separate those eyes from the main problem, I was very much up in the air. I theorized about a madman, a killer, who was seeking some priceless jewel which was concealed in a perfume bottle. The thefts of those perfume bottles had me badly baffled—until yesterday in a talk with Dr. Charlesworth, I got a clue by following which I was able to explain the thefts. In this instance, I am not going to mention any names, but I'll tell you this. On this ship there is a person who had the misfortune to contract an unusual habit, a form of drug-addiction, rare but not unheard of in medical annals. That habit was using strong perfume to produce a species of intoxication by inhaling it. If you are interested in knowing more about the vice—for a vice it is—I advise you to read certain passages in 'Against the Grain' by J. K. Huysmans. As in the case of other drugs, the habit becomes fixed, and the perfume-inhaler will do anything to get his favorite drug. It blunts the moral sensibilities of people who, normally, are straight and honorable. They will not steal money, but they will steal perfume. Now you begin to see what happened on this ship. The person I refer to—it might be any one of us—entered a number of cabins intent on finding, and purloining, perfume. When that person had some, that person was animated, lively, but without it that person was miserable and in a physical slump. I think we should not judge the perfume-user very severely. The craving gets to be well-nigh irresistible. You are wondering what perfume-using has to do with the murder of Samuel P. Cleghorn. I'll tell you."

Matthew Kelton paused, then went on.

"The time of the murder of Mr. Cleghorn, was fixed at a little after five by the fact that Larsen the steward, went to Cabin B at five in answer to a ring, and a voice, which he naturally thought belonged to Cleghorn, told him that he was not needed. If Cleghorn was able to speak at five, it followed that he had been killed some time after that hour— probably about five fifteen or twenty, as *rigor mortis* had set in when his body was discovered a few minutes after six. Since the time of the murder seemed clearly established, I felt I had something to work on—but I found that I had been working on an entirely false premise. The voice in Cabin B at five o'clock was not Cleghorn's at all. It belonged to the perfume-addict. That person had gone into Cabin B hoping to find perfume in Cleghorn's baggage. The cabin seemed empty. It was a good chance. But the cabin was not empty, for Cleghorn was lying there, dead, behind the drawn curtains of his berth. The person I shall call the addict found no perfume, but in rummaging around for it, touched, by accident, the bell which summoned the steward. Before the addict could escape from Cabin B, there was the steward knocking at the door. The addict thought quickly. Then putting on a disguised voice, the addict told the steward to go away. When he had gone, the addict got out of Cabin B, without ever knowing that a dead man was lying there. I reasoned this all out, and later secured an admission from the addict that my reasoning was correct. Now to the next step.

"Since the time of the murder was not after five, but before five, it could have taken place almost any time in the afternoon. Before I knew this, however, a gentleman present obligingly confessed that he had committed the murder. That gentleman is Mr. Sangerson, and I shall not go into the motives he declared were responsible for his act. His confession did not ring true, however. He was not sure of the time. Remember I then thought the murder had taken place after five. And he said he used a weapon which I demonstrated could not possibly have been used. Don't

frown, Mr. Sangerson. You have no cause to. I know why
you confessed the murder—"

"Why?" asked Russell Sangerson.

"For a very good reason—you were afraid someone you
loved had. Since it is certain to be known soon, I'll tell
you all that Mr. Sangerson has the good fortune to be engaged to Miss Imlay. I say 'good fortune' for in a pinch
Miss Imlay proved her quality. When she heard that Mr.
Sangerson had confessed the crime, thinking to shield her,
she immediately confessed that she was guilty, to shield
him. Her story was even more at odds with the known
facts than his. It was one of those not uncommon situ-
ations where a few minutes of candid talk would have
cleared up everything—but Mr. Sangerson and Miss Imlay did not have a chance to have that talk—for when I
announced the news of Cleghorn's murder, Miss Imlay,
fearing Mr. Sangerson was guilty, promptly fainted, and
Mr. Sangerson, knowing he wasn't guilty, attributed her
fainting to a guilty knowledge of the crime on her part.
Neither was guilty, and each was willing to take the blame
to save the other. I think we'll have to classify those two
confessions under love's labor lost.

"No, that is not accurate," went on Matthew Kelton,
"Mr. Sangerson's confession proved very useful—to me—
at any rate. For a time I half-believed it, and I went to
Captain Galvin and discussed having Mr. Sangerson arrested on suspicion. I'm afraid it was a rather shabby trick to
play on the captain. I think, though, he will forgive me,
before I have finished. When he heard that I was thinking of having Mr. Sangerson arrested, the captain himself
owned up that he had killed Cleghorn, because of an old
feud which we need not consider here. His story sounded true enough—I grant he had a strong motive for killing Cleghorn—but he told one little lie which made me
suspect that his whole account of the murder was false.

He said he had been struck by Cleghorn with a black-thorn stick—on the forearm—but I saw his forearms and there was no mark there. That may seem to some of you a minute point, but you see, I did not want to believe the captain's confession. I have my own reasons—and they're good ones—for wanting the captain to marry and enjoy a long and happy life.

"If the captain's confession was false, the next question was: why did he make it? I found the answer to that. There is a lady on this ship who was the captain's boyhood sweet-heart and a kind fate reunited them after many years of separation. She had a strong reason for killing Cleghorn, for he had done her a grave wrong years ago. When she learned from me that the captain had confessed that he killed Cleghorn, she declared that she herself had done it. I'll stop being mysterious about her identity. The lady is Miss Royd—"

They all stared at her. Kelton brought their attention back to him by saying, "Miss Royd also made one slip which made me suspect that her whole story was a fabrication. She told me she had taken a club up on deck and thrown it into the sea. I happened to run into her at a time she said she was carrying the club, and she had no club with her. Once again I suspected that some needless self-sacrificing was going on.

"This, I feel sure, was what happened. The captain saw Cleghorn come aboard and recognized him as an old ene-my whom he had known under the name of Jacob Murdo. After the ship left the pier, Captain Galvin went down to the man's cabin to have a talk with him. Entering the cabin, he found Cleghorn, or Murdo, dead, murdered. The captain, with a pardonable curiosity, examined the dead man's effects, and in his watch found a picture—probably forgotten by Murdo—of Miss Julia Royd. Captain Galvin took the picture, and went out of the cabin to do the natural thing, namely, report his discovery. But in the corridor not far from Cabin B, he encountered Miss Royd, and knew her at once. He knew that she hated Cleghorn, or Murdo, to give him his right name, and his mind jumped to the conclusion that she was responsible for his death. Now at the very moment he had that idea about her, she had a similar idea about him. For Miss Royd had also recognized Murdo when he came aboard, and had gone to his cabin just before the captain got there—and had found Murdo dead. She, too, was about to report her discovery when she saw the captain and, knowing his hate for Murdo, she at once concluded that the captain, the man she loved, had done the killing. The fact is—and I'm sure they'll both admit it now—that neither of them killed Murdo for the very simple reason that someone had been there before them. Do you see what that means? It means that bit by bit the time of the crime was pushed back from five in the afternoon, when the ship was well out at sea, to early in that day when the ship was not out at sea at all—"

There was a sudden uproar in the cabin. The ship had reached the narrow opening to Hamilton Harbor, where the channel approaches close to the shore, and land is perhaps a hundred or two hundred yards away. The cause of the uproar was the sudden vanishing of Mr. Varga. He leaped from his chair, and dashed toward the steamer rail, and was on the point of diving into the sea, when he was tackled from behind by Mr. Westervelt, and brought crashing down on the deck. Then Mr. Westervelt produced a revolver, in the business-like way of one who had done so often, and said, "No monkey business, Charley. Stay right where you are or I'll drill you."

Mr. Varga stayed where he was on the deck and his face was very ugly to look at. His black beard had come off in the struggle and he had a scarred chin. The passengers, who had rushed out of the dining saloon, clustered around the tableau. It was Detective-Sergeant Rudolph who broke the silence.

"Hello, Westervelt," he said, "what are you doing so far from home?"

"Business," said Mr. Westervelt. "This man is Charley Vaniman, alias Carlo Varga, alias Professor Garvani and a few other things, hypnotist, swindler, confidence man and general all-round crook, wanted for jobs in a lot of places but especially by us in Denver. I had a tip he was on this boat; so I tagged along. I was afraid he'd get wise and I'd lose him. That's why I played it so cautious. Lost a prisoner once by letting on I was a dick, so I made up my mind I'd take no chances this time, but would keep my trap shut, and my eyes open. I guess he got nervous just now—and tried to skip. Don't worry about this bird, Mr. Kelton. Murder isn't his line. Besides, I've had my eyes on him ever since he came on this ship, except for a few minutes when he slipped away and tried to wreck the radio set. Gosh, it's a relief to be able to be myself again. Come on, Charley. Let's have your wrists. I've a nice new pair of bracelets for them."

So saying Mr. Westervelt handcuffed the scowling Varga, and sat with him on the edge of a steamer chair.

The other passengers, shepherded by Matthew Kelton, returned to the table in the dining saloon. Not far off the white hotels and villas of Hamilton could be seen through the open door.

"I'm almost finished," said Matthew Kelton. "I've eliminated Mr. Sangerson, Miss Imlay, the captain and Miss Royd. Let me see—who's left. Keep your seats please. I'm coming back to the all-important point—the time when the murder was committed. Remember—Miss Royd went into the cabin very soon after the ship left its pier—and found Murdo already dead. When I got that point straightened out, I began to see daylight. The daylight I saw was just this: Murdo was killed before the ship left New York."

They were all watching Kelton with fascinated eyes.

"Now I have in New York a remarkable man, B. Hong by name, who has a way of finding out things. I happened to ask him the right questions, and he happened to be able to supply me with the right answers. One thing he told me. Someone came aboard—not as a passenger—but as a visitor. That person had a motive for killing Murdo, or Cleghorn. The oldest motive in the world, money. That person had stolen from Cleghorn and was about to be found out. That person killed Cleghorn a minute or two before the ship sailed, and hurried off with a crowd of other visitors. That person left behind in Cabin B a tuft of hair from his raccoon coat—and that person is sitting—there."

Kelton wheeled around and stabbed a long finger directly at Karl Roe, Cleghorn's partner.

Nobody in that cabin doubted for a second the guilt of Karl Roe. He was like a man struck by lightning. His jaws sagged open, his ruddy face turned sallow, he swallowed convulsively.

"I promised you a prisoner, Rudolph," said Kelton to the New York detective. "There he is."

Without a word, Roe held out his hands to receive the handcuffs. Then he collapsed.

"Thank God it's over," he said.

"Look at the sleeve of his fur coat," said Kelton. "See, there's a bare spot. The tuft of hair I found in Cabin B fits it exactly. Look."

"Yes," said the New York detective. "Kelton, you are a wonder."

"I'll give you a complete summary of the case, with all the evidence," said Kelton, to Rudolph, "before you sail back. You'll find that Roe has been speculating heavily in Wall Street, and I think I assumed correctly it was with embezzled money. He knew Cleghorn was about to catch him, and he knew Cleghorn would be merciless. He took a long chance, stole aboard the ship, blackjacked Cleghorn in his cabin, then mingled with the visitors leaving the ship, and was not noticed. He probably hoped that the body would not be found until the ship was well out at sea, and then one of the passengers would be suspected—perhaps Sangerson, who is really Cleghorn, or Murdo's son. Luck was with Roe for a while—he almost brought it off, but I've found that luck does not tarry long with murderers—"

"Well, I suppose you get that reward," said Detective Sergeant Rudolph.

"I'll see you get a slice of it," said Kelton. "I've a use for the rest."

"What's that?" The detective, having secured his prisoner, was paying no further attention to him.

"Most of it I'm going to turn over to the family of the dead sailor, Gabe Fest, but a little of it I'm going to save out to buy a couple of wedding presents with."

He glanced across the dining saloon. In a corner Julia Royd had her arms around her new-found son, Russell Sangerson, and Pauline Imlay and Captain Galvin stood close by.

Matthew Kelton went out into the sunlight. The S.S. *Pendragon* was almost at the Hamilton dock now. It made him uncomfortable to see people cry, even if they were crying from happiness.

17

AFTERMATH

To his hotel went Matthew Kelton in an old-fashioned open hack drawn by old-fashioned horses. It was a clear, peaceful day. At his hotel, he went at once to his room. He kneaded the bed with appreciative fingers.

"Now for a real rest," he said. "No crimes. No problems. No questions. Rest—nothing but yards and yards of rest."

He lay down on the bed and closed his eyes. He was awakened, perhaps half an hour later, by a knock on his door.

"What is it?" he called, sleepily.

"It's Mr. Galloway, the manager," a voice answered.

"What do you want?"

"I must see you, Mr. Kelton, I must, really."

"Come in," said Matthew Kelton. "Am I in the wrong room, or is the hotel afire or what is it?"

A plump little bald man minced into the room.

"You must help me, Mr. Kelton," he said. "I know you by reputation. You really must help me!"

"Help you?" inquired Matthew Kelton. "In what way can I help you, Mr. Galloway?"

"The oddest thing has happened," said the manager, "and this is a first class hotel—de luxe in fact."

"What on earth is the matter?" asked Kelton.

"Well, sir," said the manager, "a stout gentleman by the name of Mond has taken a suite on the second floor. Well, sir, it appears on the way here from the ship he stopped in at Edgerton Brothers' Emporium, our leading haberdashery, sir, and ordered a new top hat to be sent to him at this hotel by messenger at once. Well, sir, the hat arrived in its regular cardboard box not ten minutes ago—"

"Man alive, must I be kept awake to hear about Mr. Mond's hat?" demanded Kelton. "What do I care about his hat?"

"Oh, sir, it isn't the hat that I'm bothered about. It's an excellent hat. It's what Mr. Mond found in it that worries me—"

"And what was that?"

"A head," said the manager, "a man's head."

Mattew Kelton sat up in bed and sighed loudly—but there was a certain happy note in his sigh.

"I'll be with you as soon as I can slip my trousers on," said Matthew Kelton. "Now, tell me—"

THE MAY DAY MYSTERY

OCTAVUS ROY COHEN

THE STUDIO
MURDER MYSTERY
THE EDINGTONS

THE SEVEN BLACK
CHESSMEN
John Huntingdon

THE COLUMNIST
MURDER

EXTRA!

LAWRENCE SAUNDERS

COACHWHIP PUBLICATIONS

COACHWHIPBOOKS.COM

NOVEMBER JOE

DETECTIVE OF THE WOODS

H. HESKETH-PRICHARD

MURDER
IN A WALLED TOWN
KATHERINE WOODS

THE LAST TRUMPET
A HUGH RENNERT MYSTERY

TODD DOWNING

DEATH SAILS THE NILE
F. BURKS McKINLEY

COACHWHIP PUBLICATIONS

COACHWHIPBOOKS.COM

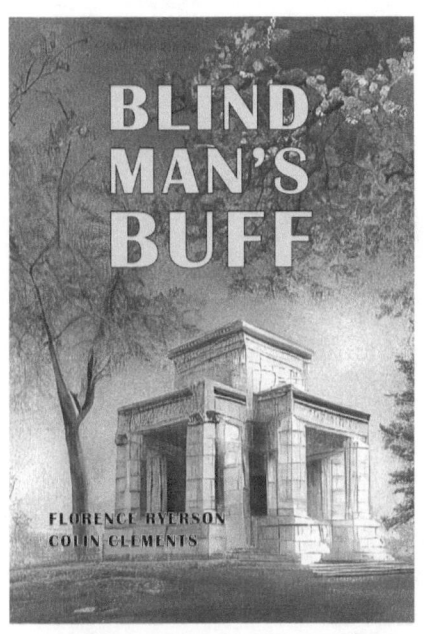

BLIND MAN'S BUFF

FLORENCE RYERSON
COLIN CLEMENTS

MURDER IN THE FAMILY

NICE PEOPLE MURDER

Mary Hastings Bradley

3 DETECTIVES
FEMMES AUDACIEUSES
MERWIN • SOMERVILLE • FOOTNER

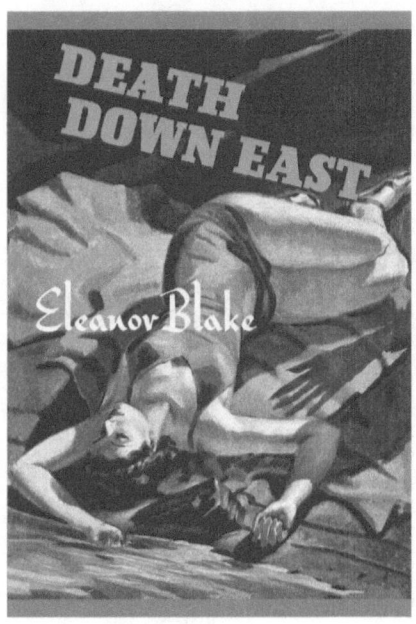

DEATH DOWN EAST

Eleanor Blake

COACHWHIP PUBLICATIONS

COACHWHIPBOOKS.COM

THE
MYSTERY
OF THE
FOLDED
PAPER

HULBERT
FOOTNER

The
Hollow Tree
Mystery

MADELON ST. DENIS

VIRGINIA RATH

FERRYMAN,
TAKE HIM ACROSS!

THE BAND PLAYED
MURDER

EDITH HOWIE

COACHWHIP PUBLICATIONS

COACHWHIPBOOKS.COM

THE QUINNY HITE
MYSTERIES

CHINESE RED · HERE LIES THE BODY

RICHARD BURKE

I'll Hate Myself in the Morning

Murder on the Left Bank

Elliot Paul

MURDER'S COMING

GRAVE WITHOUT GRASS

BY
DONALD CLOUGH CAMERON

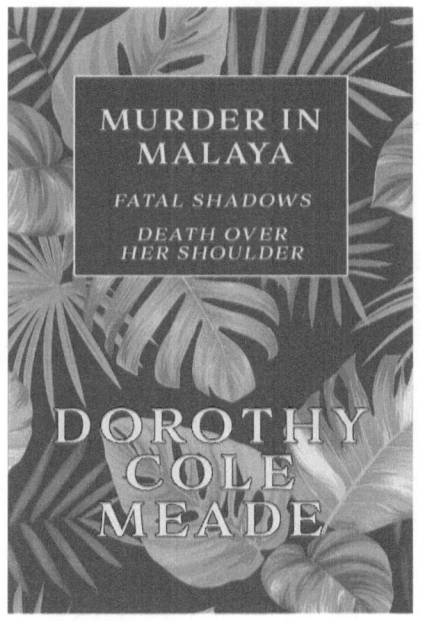

MURDER IN
MALAYA

FATAL SHADOWS

DEATH OVER
HER SHOULDER

DOROTHY
COLE
MEADE

COACHWHIP PUBLICATIONS

COACHWHIPBOOKS.COM

COACHWHIP PUBLICATIONS

COACHWHIPBOOKS.COM

THE FIRES AT
FITCH'S FOLLY

KENNETH WHIPPLE

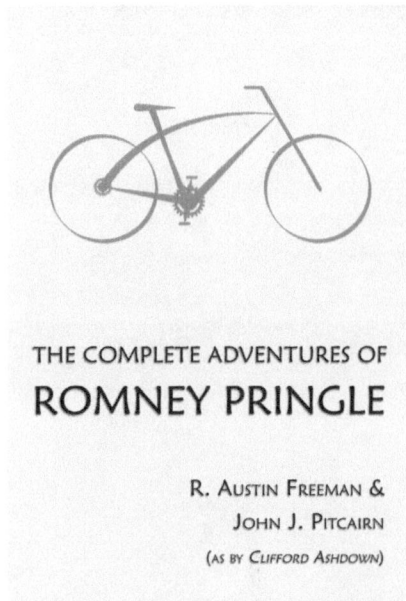

THE COMPLETE ADVENTURES OF
ROMNEY PRINGLE

R. AUSTIN FREEMAN &
JOHN J. PITCAIRN
(AS BY CLIFFORD ASHDOWN)

GRIMM
DEATH

THE
GROUSE
MOOR
MURDER

JOHN FERGUSON

COACHWHIP PUBLICATIONS

COACHWHIPBOOKS.COM

www.ingramcontent.com/pod-product-compliance
Lightning Source LLC
Chambersburg PA
CBHW020602250626
47154CB00004B/1334